Woods Wall

Mac Travis Adventures

Steven Becker

STEVEN BECKER

* * *

Join my mailing list
and get a free copy of Wood's Ledge
http://mactravisbooks.com

Chapter 1

Pete looked over his shoulder at the spread. The fishing lines glistened in the sun as they trailed behind the twenty-four-foot boat trolling southwest through the light chop of the Gulfstream. The wind was light, the water glassy with a gentle swell. Satisfied the lines were running true, he returned his focus to the water. He looked over at his friends, lulled into a state of semi-consciousness by the motion of the boat and the beers they'd drank. They'd been hammering beers all day. He wondered how it had taken this long for them to pass out. It'd been a good day with plenty of Mahi Mahi in the fish box. He was thinking about calling it a day and heading back in.

"Birds at one o'clock!" he yelled. He had been scanning the water for any sign of life; birds and debris were the ticket for bait which led to bigger fish. Dan and Jeff popped awake. "C'mon guys -- one more -- let's go." Pete steered toward the birds while Jeff checked the lines. The three friends had fished together long enough that they had the smoothness of a well-oiled machine, each knowing their jobs. The boat moved closer to the birds, clearly working some bait on the surface. The three men watched as the birds crashed and soared, intent on the bait below, as the boat pulled through the bait pod.

The clicker buzzed as one of the reels gave line. "Fish on!" Pete continued the course and speed to set the hook and see if they could get another fish to hit one of the four remaining baits. "It's pretty good size. Let's pull in the other lines."

Dan grabbed the rod with the fish and held it high to keep it clear of the other lines. He left the drag loose, letting the fish take some line off as Jeff brought in the rods. Pete circled the boat around as Dan reeled. The fish jumped, revealing itself, then crashed and sounded. Dan continued to bring in line. The fish was close now but was startled when it saw the boat and pulled harder, the drag whizzing as line came off the reel. Dan let it run, sweat dripping from his brow, waiting for the inevitable as the fish jumped and crashed sideways into the water, irritated by the hook and the pull of the line. This was the crux of the fight. The fish would soon lose energy.

They went back and forth, the fish jumping, Dan patiently bringing it closer. "He's ready!" he finally yelled.

At that, Jeff grabbed the gaff and stood by Dan at the side of the boat as Pete drove, watching the water; keeping the fish parallel with the boat. The boat moved slowly through the water, the exhausted fish, its electric blue color now half-green with fatigue, slid next to the boat. Jeff lowered the gaff into the water and, with a swift pull, set the point into the fish. He hefted it quickly onto the boat, and then into the waiting fish box, and the struggle was over.

"Damn boys! Must go a little over thirty pounds," Dan said as he closed the box and offered up a round of beers. High fives and can tabs popping marked the end of the bout.

* * *

They were stowing gear and spraying off the deck, removing the fish blood before the tropical sun baked it on the deck. "Give it another pass?" Pete asked.

"Something in the water over there!" Jeff called out, pointing to the starboard side of the boat. Pete scanned the water, following Jeff's gaze. He changed course and directed the boat toward the object bobbing in the waves. Debris was common in the Gulf Stream, and a great fish attractant. In their experience, anything in the water could hold fish, even something as small as a crab trap buoy with a piece of line attached might hold fish.

The object took shape as they got closer, the sun reflecting off the brown plastic, shining in the sun, wrapped tight around a square object.

"That's not trash," Dan said from the bow. They were fifty feet from it, but it was already obvious that they were looking at something more than a crab trap or piece of flotsam. "Looks fresh in the water, too. Let's grab it and see what it is."

Pete slowed the engine and coasted up to the package. Maybe two feet square, it hadn't been in the water long. Dan leaned over the gunwale and gaffed the package. He struggled with the weight to get it over the side. Finally it landed on the deck and sat there, undisturbed. The three fishermen stared at it.

"That's a square grouper. Let's open it and see what we've got," Jeff said.

"Make it quick," Pete said, scanning the horizon. The level-headed one of the group, he wasn't seeing this as treasure, but as danger. If it was out here, someone was looking for it. Waterproofed packages didn't just appear in the Gulf Stream.

Jeff slid the knife through the outer wrapping, opening it to reveal white paper known as house wrap in the home building industry. As the waterproof fabric opened, small bundles individually wrapped in brown plastic revealed themselves. The size of bricks, neatly stacked, they spilt onto the deck.

"Open one up," Dan said, excited at the prospect. "It's either drugs or money." He reached for a brick.

"We ought to throw them back. This looks like trouble to me." Pete continued to scan the horizon.

"Oh calm down, you freakin' pussy. Figures you're an insurance guy. This has been in the water overnight at least. There's no one here." Dan slit one open, ignoring his friend. "Yes." He held up the opened package for Jeff and Dan to see. Cocaine sparkled in the sunlight. He brought it down to examine it. The white powder, caked into a brick had the initials DV pressed

5

into it.

Pete leaned over Dan's shoulder, staring intently at the item. "Well, whoever DV is, he's gonna want this back," he said. Before he could say anything else, he was interrupted by the radio.

"*Coastguard Station Key West to....*" Pete jumped and scooped several bricks into his arms. He was about to start tossing bricks back in.

But Jeff stopped him. "There's no one here. The radio call was *not* about us. Calm down and let's figure out what to do here."

"Party is what we do here," Dan said. He took a knife and carved a corner of the brick. Powder fell off onto the blade, and he raised it to his nose and snorted. He laid his head back waiting for the drug to take effect. "Whoa, that's amazing." He passed the knife to Jeff.

Several long minutes passed as they sat on the deck, staring at the bundles. Dan had counted and stacked them into ten piles of five bricks, each about a pound. Jeff, the numbers guy, tried to do the math in his head, breaking the pounds to ounces, then to grams, multiplying by one hundred - the street price for a gram. In the end, though, the calculation was too much for the number of beers he'd consumed. He just shrugged, saying that whatever it was, that much cocaine was worth a lot of money.

"We gotta move." Pete said as he scanned the horizon.

Four boats were coming at them. Not that it was any surprise; any boat sitting still in the Gulf Stream was like a magnet. Other boats thought they were hooked up and headed toward them, hoping to draw the school of fish away ... or at least pick up a straggler. The boats were getting closer, some running at full speed. Two of the boats were clearly fishing charters, their fly bridges visible from a distance. Another smaller fishing boat's outriggers dipped, almost hitting the waves, as it cruised towards them. The last boat was different. A custom paint job, yellow hull with red highlights, its shape that of a cigarette boat.

All three men were starring at the racing boat now. "Get some baits out. Start trolling," Pete said as he set the boat in gear and steered a course away from the yellow boat. "They all think we're on fish and that cigarette boat doesn't look like he's got a rod on it."

The fishing boats turned away as soon as they saw the boat deploy lines and resume trolling. Whatever they thought might be there was probably gone. The yellow boat maintained it's collision course.

"Cover that thing." Pete yelled.

Dan and Jeff grabbed the bricks and tossed them into the fish cooler. They had just stuffed the packaging into the trash bin when the boats passed, only feet separating them. A tall dark skinned man eyed each of them individually, then scanned the boat. He made a pistol with his fingers and fired an imaginary shot at them. Satisfied he pressed down on the throttle and moved on. A collective sigh came from the men.

"That's one scary dude - and you know what he was looking for," Pete said.

"Well, he's gone now." Dan said as he went for the cooler and grabbed the open brick. He huddled with Jeff again each snorting off the knife.

"He knows what we look like. I say we toss all this and call it a good fishing day. Nothing but trouble's going to come out of keeping it," Pete said hoping the others would agree.

"No, don't think so," Dan said as he looked at Jeff who was nodding in agreement.

The two men repacked the bricks in the fish box, below the ice, and covered it with fish.

Chapter 2

Two women came through the sliding glass door of the rented house as the boat pulled up to the dock. They wore bikini tops and shorts; each carried a tall glass. Pete waved at them and wondered how many they'd had. "Think we can keep this quiet?" he asked Dan and Jeff. Silence answered his question as they finished their beers.

"You boys got dinner?" Penny asked. "It's kind of late."

"Yeah and then some," Dan responded. Pete tried to stare him down. "We did well. How about mixing us a couple of those?" He gestured to the drinks.

"Sure thing, hun." The girls went back toward the air-conditioned house.

The women were barely out of hearing range when Pete whirled on Dan, furious. "Dammit. We're not back thirty seconds, and you have to start laying on innuendoes. Can you please keep this quiet until we figure out what to do with it," Pete pleaded. He looked at Dan carefully, noting that he was grinding his jaw and his pupils were dilated. "How much of that did you do, anyhow? You're a mess." Pete regretted picking up the package. There was no telling what Dan was going to do.

"Never mind," Jeff said. "He's okay, probably just needs a couple of drinks to take the edge off."

"Well, I'm gonna grab the cooler from the carport. We've got to get this off the boat before anyone sees. I don't know about you guys, but that guy in the cigarette boat scared the crap out of me."

As Pete walked away, Jeff and Dan looked at each other.

Then, without saying anything, each grabbed a brick and put it in their backpacks.

"Getting laid tonight," Dan muttered, smiling. They high-fived and set the packs to the side. "Screw him."

Pete returned with the empty cooler. He set it next to the fish box, neatly stacking and counting the bricks as he set them in. Dan and Jeff provided cover by unloading the fish onto the dock. Suddenly the sliding glass door opened, the sound startling Pete so much that he lost count around forty. As the girls approached, he quickly finished his work and closed the lid.

At that point, Dan made a production of laying out the day's catch, hoping to distract them. The women did the "ooh, ah" thing, as expected, and Dan told them how they'd caught the fish, embellishing each story. "Help me with this," Pete called to Jeff as he lifted the cooler onto the dock.

The house was built on concrete piers to protect it from the storm surge brought by hurricanes. Although not permissible by the building code, most houses had small apartments and storerooms built underneath them. They carried the cooler each with a hand on a handle into the cluttered room. Jeff started moving gear until a space opened in the corner. They set the cooler there and carefully used the gear to hide it.

"You've got to get a handle on Dan," Pete said as they finished. "He's blown out of his mind. He won't listen to me, but maybe he'll listen to you."

"I can see that. You know how he gets when he wants to party — there's no stopping him. Donna will be right there with him, too."

"And what about you?" Pete asked.

"I had a little but haven't touched that stuff in years. Got no desire," Jeff lied, imagining the all-night scene he hoped would play out in the bedroom later.

Pete looked over at him, "What do you think we should do with it?"

"I'd say we've got a couple options - and dumping it's not one of them. I know it scares you, hell, scares me too - but it's a major score. We can't just pass it up. I know a guy back in Tampa who might be able to help out."

"I don't know." Scenarios ran through Pete's mind - none of them good. "It'll be like having a dead body in the garage, having that stuff around."

"Let's sleep on it and talk tomorrow. We've got fish to clean."

* * *

Cesar pulled the cigarette boat up to the seawall. In neutral, the boat stopped in place at the dock, held in place by the wind. He tied off, grabbed his cell phone, and headed for his truck.

The heat from the truck hit him as he opened the door. He reached in, turned on the ignition and opened all the windows to let the air blast for a few minutes waiting for the super-heated interior to cool before he got in. The truck cooled quickly, and he got in, dreading the call he needed to make. The truck was cool now, but sweat continued to drip from his brow. He picked up his phone and noticed there was a text from Diego, received over an hour ago; no content, just a signal to call back. It could only mean one thing, and Cesar was terrified of the repercussions.

He drove the two miles to his house in a panic, wondering how to explain this to Diego. He pulled in the driveway, got out and let himself into his house. In the hallway, he pulled down the attic access ladder and climbed several rungs until he could reach his hand under the insulation. The baggie was there, just where he'd left it. Inside was another cell phone — a burner, prepaid and untraceable. He went to the recent calls screen and pushed Diego's number.

Three rings, four rings … he waited patiently, hoping for voicemail when the sound changed. His hopes were dashed when the line suddenly connected.

"Yeah. You got it, *mi hermano*?"

Cesar took a deep breath. Now came the part he'd been dreading. "We got a problem. I got four of them. The fifth wasn't there. I can't pick up a signal from the beacon, either. I've been out all day looking, but there're so many fishing boats, I can't search without looking suspicious."

There was a long, toxic pause on the other end, and Cesar closed his eyes. Diego was one of the most powerful men in Mexico, and Cesar had spent most of his life fearing the drug lord. It had been chance that led him to this position as runner, and there were times when he wished he'd become a sugar cane farmer instead.

Now was one of those moments.

"Was it the special package?" his boss asked, his voice dangerously quiet.

This was the question Cesar had feared most. "Yes, *patron*."

He could almost see the scene on the other end of the phone. Diego was infamous for his temper and what he did with it. Scarface had nothing on the trail of bodies tied to him. If he wanted, he could end Cesar's life - and every member of his family's.

When he spoke again, he emphasized each word. "Find it, Cesar. Or you, and all you hold dear, will die." He paused, "I don't think I need to tell you how."

"Yes, *patron*," Cesar mumbled.

The call disconnected and Cesar put the phone down, his hand shaking. No, Diego didn't need to tell him how he would die. He'd seen it before, when men had failed the drug lord. Their screams still haunted his dreams.

He replaced the phone, went to the refrigerator and put his hand toward a cold beer. Changing his mind, he quickly moved it to a bottle of water. Alcohol was no cure for the disease he now carried.

Chapter 3

Pete wanted nothing more than his bed, but the party at the house was in high gear for Dan, Jeff, and the girls. Music was loud and hips were grinding while he looked on, planning his exit strategy. The only single one of the group, he didn't often feel like a fifth wheel. Except when they were partying.

He rubbed the callus on the base of his ring finger. Regret about his situation didn't visit often, but when it did, the melancholy was unbearable. Divorced for three years, he was lonelier than he would admit to himself. He watched the couples interact with each other and saw through the effects of the drugs and alcohol. He saw the connections. Realizing there was no rest to be had here, he decided on a change of scenery.

Unnoticed, he slid from the room and out the front door. He looked at the car, but chose the bicycle instead. Although nowhere near the level of intoxication of his friends, he'd had a few, and didn't want to risk it. A DUI would totally screw his custody situation.

He pedaled out of the driveway, wobbly at first, but quickly gaining confidence. Maybe he'd had more to drink than he thought. He rode through the neighborhood and turned left at Sombrero Golf Course, heading towards the Dockside bar. He glanced at the boats moored at the seawall, most dark and empty, wondering if he might have to crash on one. The bar was half full when he entered; a solo guitar player strumming Jimmy Buffet covers was the only one who looked at him - showing him where the tip jar was with a nod. He sat down at the bar, as far away from the crowd as he could get and ordered a beer. The barmaid set the cold bottle in front of him. He lifted it, took a sip and sat back as he reflected on the day's events and wondered how he could stop his out of control friends from getting them all killed. He could sneak back and dump the drugs in the canal while they were all partying, but he feared Dan's reaction ... especially if he were still high when he found out.

The bar was filling up, nine o'clock Saturday night and things were getting into gear. He felt alone, sitting by himself, nursing a beer. A rotund tourist and his equally rotund wife vacated the seats next to him. Hoping they would be filled by someone he could talk to, he slowly sipped his beer.

The teeth were the first thing he saw. Way too large for the face that presented them, whiter than any middle-aged man's teeth should be. Even the tall frame and long hair couldn't disguise the size of the grill in his mouth. Fifty-seven Chevy came to mind as the man pulled out the stool and sat down.

The barmaid pecked the man's cheek over the bar and placed a cold beer in front of him without asking. *Not only a guy, but a local,* Pete thought. Great. He took a big sip of his beer, thinking about escaping from here too. Then he took another gulp and coughed, beer spewing from his mouth.

"Easy there, partner." The big guy signaled the barmaid for a glass of water. "You okay, there? No need to be rushing things."

Pete collected himself, blood rushing to his face in embarrassment. "Yeah, I'm good. Thanks."

"No problem. Name's Alan, but most call me Tru, short for Trufante."

"Pete." He extended his hand.

"No worries, man. Let's get you another beer and settle ya down." He picked up the bottle, "More backwash in that than beer." Trufante called down the bar, and a fresh, cold beer arrived a moment later.

They sat quietly for a few minutes, each enjoying his space. Pete was grateful for the silence, not really wanting to get in a discussion with a local. Locals and tourists didn't often mix well.

He watched as Trufante smiled again as the door opened and an attractive brunette dressed in scrubs walked in. With a sigh he turned away as the woman approached, clearly making for Trufante.

Trufante got up and placed her between his stool and Pete's. They kissed rabidly, then turned to Pete.

"Sue, this is Pete. He's down here looking a little out of sorts."

"Hey, good to meet you. You down here by yourself?" she asked, looking Pete up and down.

"Fishing with a couple of buddies who brought their wives. Started feeling like a fifth wheel, so I came down here," he mumbled.

"Hey, what about we set him up with Joanie?" Sue said, turning to Trufante. "She's feeling a little down. Maybe head down to Key West."

"Sweet." The smile lit up his face again as Pete wondered what he had walked into.

"Maybe I ought to just head home."

"No way dude," Sue said. We're gonna fix you up and I'm not taking no for an answer."

* * *

An hour later, Pete was in love. The backseat of Sue's Camry was just small enough to initiate body contact every time she hit a pothole. And Joanie giggled every time they touched. Pete thought it a nervous thing, but kind of cute anyway. The rest of her was cute to match. Petite, with red hair and some scattered freckles, even on the top of her cleavage, which was displayed by her low-cut top. He was entranced, as they jiggled with every bump. She didn't talk much, though, just giggled and jiggled.

Sue found a parking spot a few blocks off Duval Street, and they headed toward the noise of Saturday night, Trufante and Sue several steps ahead. Pete felt Joanie intertwine her fingers with his. His hand almost moved away as his heart jumped at the touch. But he smiled and relaxed.

They settled into a rhythm of drinking and dancing and, at some point, he realized that Trufante had disappeared. Pete didn't notice until he found himself dancing with two women. It was the stuff of dreams; he looked around for Trufante's six foot plus frame and smile. He didn't see him anywhere. Sue and Joanie sandwiched him and started grinding, and soon all else was forgotten.

They were back at the bar, Pete ordering drinks for the girls and one for himself that he probably didn't need when Trufante strutted back in, grin a little wider, if that were possible. Pete saw him hand something to Sue as he hugged her. Seconds later, the girls made a beeline toward the lady's room.

"Got some stuff if you want to keep partying." Trufante leaned into him so he could hear over the music.

"No, that's okay, thanks. I really like that girl, though. Can't thank you guys enough."

"No worries." Trufante slapped Pete's back.

Something was pinging in his head, though. Trufante seemed to be well known and connected here. He obviously knew where to score, and seemed pretty nonchalant about it.

Chapter 4

Cleaning his gun calmed him. It was like meditation — the ritual, the order. Always the same, no thought. Cesar liked the routine, the smell of gun oil and gunpowder. The feel of cold, clean steel.

He sat in the kitchen, the house quiet, noise filtering in from the street. The proximity to Duval Street was a double-edged sword — good for business, bad for quiet. Cleaning the guns settled him. Something he needed especially now, when he needed to think.

He'd had several visitors tonight. A little slow for a Saturday, but it was still early. He glanced at his watch. Not even midnight yet. The gun reassembled, he put the cleaning materials away and loaded it. Then he settled into his chair by the door, reached underneath, and placed the gun in the holster fastened there.

The opaque curtains next to him filtered the street light, but allowed him to see ghost-like images of the foot traffic. The curtains were a compromise. He needed privacy, but also needed to see if anyone was approaching the house. In his line of business, surprises were not welcome. He reached over for the TV clicker and turned on a soccer game.

He couldn't concentrate on the game, though. Diego and the missing package weighed heavily on his mind. He'd grown up with the man in the Tabasco region of southern Mexico. Always underneath him in the cartel structure, he'd witnessed his violence many times, fortunately never being on the receiving end. The idea that he might be the victim this time terrified him.

The chime for a new text message startled him from his

thoughts. He looked down at the phone, read the message, and typed OK in response, hoping it would be a big sale. He had some time to kill before the deal. At his computer he went to the NOAA website and found the ocean current screen. He entered the coordinates for the drop from memory. The screen showed an icon one mile southwest of Wood's Wall. If he could calculate the current and wind, he might be able to establish a search area. Cruising aimlessly in the Gulf Stream was not going to do anything but waste gas. He stared at the wavy lines on the screen in vain.

The drop was in the Gulf Stream, the huge ocean current running up the North American coast, like a river running North in the middle of the ocean. It didn't take a rocket scientist to calculate the current running at six mph times twenty-four hours. The package could be two hundred miles north by now, past Palm Beach. Without the locator, it could ride the swift current of the Gulf Stream for another week, ending up somewhere near Greenland, and they'd have no way of finding it. He sat back and put his head in his hands. The search area was huge.

* * *

Pete was entranced with giggles and jiggles on the way back from Key West, as Sue slowed through Big Pine Key, the biggest speed trap in the Keys, and maybe the country. The entire island was a protected area for the Key Deer; the speed limit dropped to thirty-five miles per hour at night. It wasn't a question of *if* there was a state trooper waiting; it was more a question of how many. You could get away with a little swerve here and there as long as the speed stayed down. There were always enough speeders to keep the cops busy and the drunk tank full.

Once over the bridge, though, the speed limit picked back up to fifty-five. At that rate, Pete figured he only had about fifteen minutes before they reached Marathon. It was pretty much now or never for those freckles. He was hesitant, but she made it easy for him as he moved towards her. They kissed the length of the Seven Mile Bridge "Where should we drop you?" The voice snapped him back to reality.

"He's going with me. Don't y'all worry," Joanie said.

The parking lot of the bar was deserted when they pulled in. The couple in the backseat disengaged and exited their separate doors, only to reengage as soon as they were out of the car. Then, just as the car was about to pull away, Pete ran up to the driver's side window.

"Let me get your number," he said to Trufante. "I've got something that can maybe help us both out."

Trufante smiled and recited the digits while Pete punched them in his phone.

* * *

It was seventy-nine degrees at five am. Mel looked at the thermometer in disgust as she headed out the door of her Georgetown apartment. Clad only in a sports bra and running shorts, water bottle in hand and cell phone in a band on her arm, she set off at a slow jog. It didn't take long for sweat to start beading on her forehead as her stride loosened in the early morning heat and humidity. Twenty minutes later, she arrived at the boathouse on the Potomac River.

Outrigger canoeing had quickly become her new passion. Her boyfriend, Mac Travis had introduced her to stand-up paddle boarding in the Keys. Though she liked it, she was more of a team player and had joined the outrigger club on her return. The combination of technique in the stroke, along with the endurance, power, and camaraderie had come together and ignited her.

Even at this early hour, the boathouse was busy. The sun had risen half an hour earlier, the water glistening in its rays. Rowers and paddlers tended to prefer the early morning, as the wind was calmer, the water flatter, and — most importantly — there was an absence of speed boaters. In the middle of the day on a hot Sunday in May, the river would be entangled with all sorts of watercraft in a few hours. In the early morning, though, it was relatively deserted.

She watched as several rowing shells moved out into the calm water, excited as the crew assembled. Their combined passion about training and racing had placed them in the top three of the early season race series.

She set her phone down on a pile of their belongings, uncharacteristically without a glance at the screen, and they all headed for the canoe. Once on the water, they quickly assembled the ama, the outrigger that stabilized the boat, and set out, their paddles synchronous in the water, each member working hard to match the stroke of the lead paddler.

Their stroke rate and intensity increased after ten minutes. The canoe moved quickly through the water as the paddle blades reached out and grabbed water. The only sound was the *Hut* and *Ho* every fifteen strokes, as the paddlers changed sides. The pace lasted for a brutal thirty minutes before they took a water break and turned back towards the boathouse.

* * *

An hour later, as the sun was gaining altitude, the sweat covered paddlers exited the water and returned the canoe to its place. Then, plans made for the next session, they headed their separate ways.

Mel went for her phone first and saw the two texts and three missed calls, all from her boss. *Really,* she thought, *this time on a Sunday morning, what could be so damned important?* She was trying to extricate herself from the web of Davies and Associates, and this latest example of her boss's neediness was just one more reason. The passion was all but gone, and the spotlight and large paychecks no longer compensated for the lack of that zeal she'd previously felt toward their causes. But really, she knew, it wasn't the job so much as it was Mac.

She drank from her water bottle, trying to decide if she should get home, shower, and put on her lawyer skin before calling back. Conscience overcame her though, and she sat down, scrolled to the recent call screen, and pressed the name.

She listened intently as her boss spoke, her brow furrowing as she became engrossed in the conversation. After listening for several minutes, she asked several quick questions and ended the call with a promise to meet at a local coffee shop in an hour. Her Sunday now ruined, she put the phone back in the armband, grabbed her water bottle and headed up the hill toward her apartment. She moved faster now, anger replacing the elated feeling from the paddle.

Chapter 5

The sun was glaring through the window when Pete woke, Joanie purring beside him. He watched her sleep for a few minutes before getting out of bed. She had brought some things out in him last night that he thought were buried forever. He hoped last night's partying was not the norm for her. That would be a deal breaker if she was into that scene.

He dressed quietly, doing his best not to wake her. In the kitchen he found a pen and a notepad and sat down to leave a note. He agonized for several long minutes about whether to leave her his phone number or if it were better to just say thank you and disappear. Settled on the phone number and then, a moment of panic, wondering if she would call, he left with a smile. Downstairs, he stayed in the shade of the building. The sun was high, temperature pushing ninety. Relief washed over him as he turned on his phone and saw no notifications on the screen. At least nothing bad had happened with Dan and Jeff last night he thought. The memory of the night before was replaced by trepidation about the drugs. They had to go. It was only a matter of time before Dan would do something stupid. Why not give Trufante a shot at it. His number was in the notepad app where he'd left it last night. He copied the number into his key pad and hit call.

Trufante answered on the fourth ring. "Huh."

"Tru, it's Pete, from last night."

"Hey." He'd clearly been asleep, and wasn't ready for a conversation, but Pete jumped in anyhow. Better now than never, and the sooner he could move that package they'd picked up, the sooner he could get on with his life.

"Listen, I need to talk to you."

"Dude, it's early."

Pete looked at the sun, surprised that it was near it's apex. "This could make us both a lot of money."

There was a pause, and then: "Well, it's not *that* early. What's up?"

"Pick me up at Joanie's and I'll lay it out for you."

"Got to get these old bones moving. Be there in a few."

Pete waited by the road, wondering about his fortune. He hadn't thought this through as much as he'd have liked. Usually a methodical person, the kind of guy who listed the pros and cons on a piece of paper before making a decision, he'd gone off the tracks. A party night in Key West and now trying to offload a ton of coke to someone he barely knew was not his style; he felt adrenaline running through him, experiencing things he'd never felt before. First Joanie last night and now the unknown feeling of a deal about to go down. He didn't know what it was, but he kind of liked it. Phone still in hand he opened the calculator and did some quick math while he waited. Fifty pounds at sixteen ounces each was eight hundred ounces at twenty-eight grams each was twenty-two thousand four hundred grams -- at a hundred each -- he looked at the screen and staggered backwards. Sold off by the gram their package was worth over two million dollars.

After about ten minutes, Trufante pulled up in Sue's Camry. "You know they've got taxi's here," he muttered no sign of the signature smile.

"It's not just a ride I need." There was a pregnant pause. He was unsure how to start, but noticed Trufante getting antsy. "Listen, me and some buddies found a square grouper yesterday -- coke."

"No shit. Hop on in." Trufante was wide awake now. "I'm

guessing you brought it back or you wouldn't be talking now. How much you say you got?"

"There were fifty packages. Probably about a pound each."

"Describe the wrapping, everything you can think of."

Pete leaned back in the seat and closed his eyes as he recalled the package. He described the outer wrapping, the inner wrapping, and how the bricks were individually wrapped and stacked. The initials embossed on the powder got a quick reaction.

"DV? You're sure about that?"

"Yeah, why?"

"Got an idea I know who that might belong to. No transmitter or any electronics on it?"

Pete answered in the negative, and Trufante nodded.

"Real unusual for them to drop that much without a transmitter. Must have fallen off." He scratched the two-day-old stubble on his face and rubbed his eyes. "What kind of idea you got that might involve me?"

"I was just thinking that it might be easier to get rid of it down here than to take it home. A lot safer, anyway."

Trufante shook his head, his face suddenly serious, and Pete's heart dropped. "There's nothing safe about what you got. I'll guarantee there's some mean-ass folks looking for you guys right now." It was quiet for a few minutes while Pete tried to engage his brain.

Finally Trufante sighed. "Got an idea that might work. Make all of us look good. Thing is, you're not going to get what you think for it. You get greedy with this thing, it's not going to go well for you guys."

"I'm open. It's pure profit anyway. We just got lucky."

"Let's not call it lucky 'til you're back home with the cash stuffed in your mattress. I think I know whose those initials are. If it's his stuff, we just return it and trust his generosity for a reward. We all look good and get some cash."

Pete was silent. He was sure Dan had a number in his head ... probably breaking the whole thing into grams and selling it like that ... over a half million each. That was how the alphabet agencies gave street value -- the lowest salable amounts brought in the most money. Selling it off in grams at a hundred bucks a shot would net much more than a reward. But the risks of doing that were astronomical. One or all of them winding up dead or in jail was not a long shot. This made sense to his logical mind. Just take the reward. "What would you be expecting out of this?"

"I set up the whole deal. You and me take it together. I don't want to meet your buddies. Cut me in for a full share and I'm good."

Pete held out his hand. "I got to sell this to my buddies. But they don't really have a choice. They might be dreaming of getting rich off this, but they have no way to sell it. I'll talk them into it. Okay, four-way split."

Trufante ignored the hand. "Put that away, this ain't no business deal."

* * *

Mel sat at the coffee house, waiting for her boss to show. She thumbed her phone, rubbing the edges, trying to make it vibrate. She hadn't heard from Mac, her boyfriend in Marathon, for at least a day. Not all that unusual for him. She knew that. He lived in a different world without the constant text messages ... and no Facebook or Twitter. She doubted he even knew what they were. It had been an hour since she'd received the message from her boss. She'd showered, packed, and gotten to their meeting. And now he was late. Typical.

She was so engrossed in massaging her phone that she didn't notice him come in until he sat down. She looked up and smiled to herself; he could have been her grandfather in a track suit. And in many ways, he was. Bradley Davies had found Mel, fresh out of law school, full of radical ideas and the energy to see them through. He'd immediately become a mentor -- channeling that energy into his causes.

"Sorry for the quick notice. This just came up Friday night, and no one was in the office yesterday." He handed her a sheaf of papers, then waited patiently while she scanned them.

"Sons of bitches. Tried to pull the Friday afternoon fast ball. Slide in a hearing on Friday afternoon for Monday morning, hoping we wouldn't get there."

"Pretty much. I went in this morning to check on something else and saw this on the fax machine."

"I can prepare on the plane. Not a big deal, just a discovery hearing. Those bastards are trying to disallow my testimony as an eyewitness, due to a conflict of interest."

She sat back, thinking. She'd seen what the US Navy had done first hand ... used drones to spy on her father. Using drones to spy on US citizens on US soil was highly illegal.

"I think you might want to step aside and just play the witness here," Davies said suddenly.

Mel shook her head sharply. "I've been lead council on this suit from the start. No way I'm stepping aside. Even if they disallow my testimony, Mac was there with me. *He'll* testify."

The overgrown grey eyebrows furrowed at the mention of Mac's name. "Will he?"

"For me he will," Mel said, though she hesitated slightly. Mac leaned toward being invisible. He was a libertarian, much like her father had been. Neither liked the way the government meddled in their lives. She'd thought her dad, always a conspiracy buff, was just paranoid until she witnessed firsthand how corrupt the men and women in power actually were. At one point she had aspired to be one of them; now she just wanted to stop them.

"Look, you're not going to like this, but I'm sending Jason Patel down there to back you up."

"Damn it, I have my own team! You know I can't stand that

guy. He's a freakin suck up."

"He does what I ask him to do." He leaned forward. "Look, Mel, I love you like a daughter, but you've changed. You're on a mission to avenge your father. I understand it, but it's not always aligned with our purpose. You used to be the cheerleader. Now … well, you've changed. Patel will do a good job."

Finally she sighed. "I don't have a choice, do I?"

"I'm afraid not, kiddo."

They got up and hugged. "Be careful down there. You have some enemies."

Chapter 6

Pete looked around the house in disbelief. It looked like a scene from Caligula. Four unconscious, half-dressed bodies were strewn among the cushions pulled off the couches. Liquor bottles, mostly empty, sat on the coffee table. A pile of white powder was piled on the glass of a picture taken from the wall. An open brick lay on the kitchen counter.

He panicked and went for the storeroom. The gear they had used to hide the cooler looked untouched. They were either really careful or had taken the brick out on the boat and hid it. He remembered losing count as they loaded them into the cooler. There were fifty when they were laid on the deck of the boat -- how many were left in the cooler? He remembered counting to at least forty before he got distracted.

He moved the surrounding gear and stared at the cooler. He opened the lid; it looked the same. One by one, he took the bricks out of the cooler, and started to stack them. Sweat poured down his brow from the heat in the enclosed space.

He had four stacks of ten laid out when he removed the last bricks. At five, he realized they were short. Forty-eight. He double-checked his count as he replaced them, and paused when he noticed that one package was slightly different. It was hard and slightly smaller. He hadn't noticed anything different before, but he hadn't handled every one - Jeff had helped him. It was slightly smaller but had the same outer wrapping. Curious, he removed a corner of the wrapping, and saw the dull sheen of metal.

He placed the unusual brick to the side and loaded the cooler again. His brain was swirling - working on full power now — the missing inventory made him sure that his friends, now partners, had liberated a brick each for themselves. If it came up, he would confront them and say he took a brick to even things up. The gear back in place he went back to the house.

He passed the couples still prone on the floor, pausing to make sure each was still breathing. Satisfied he went to his room and stashed the brick in the closet. Back in the living room he surveyed the scene again, trying to decide whether to wake the dead. The wind was down, and it would be another good fishing day, though they'd get a late start. In the end, he decided to load the boat and then wake them. The open water would be a good spot for privacy. They needed to have a board meeting, away from the women, so he could sell them on his plan.

* * *

Dan and Jeff looked green before they even left the dock, and Pete relished the payback as he watched them, surprised that both held onto the contents of their stomachs - sure that he wouldn't be able to if he'd partied like that. They'd only agreed to go after they each had another line from the mountain of drugs on the coffee table. He doubted whether it had helped much. Now, he continued the torture as he took his time bringing the boat on plane, letting it pound a few more waves before accelerating. Before long, Dan and Jeff were starting to nod off, succumbing to the rhythm of the boat as they made their way to the Gulf Stream, twelve miles off the reef.

Pete slowed as they approached a weed patch. He yelled for Dan and Jeff to get up and get lines in the water. Frustrated at their lack of response he set the boat in neutral and started to set out two rods himself. As soon as the second line was out he went back to the helm and nudged the throttle forward, slowly moving the boat towards the weeds.

The reel screamed as line came off it - a fish jumping fifty feet off the boat. The alarm woke Dan and Jeff who instantly went for the rods. The fish came in easily. It was a schoolie, just longer than the twenty-inch limit. The school swarmed around the boat after following their lost comrade. Ordinarily they would have kept the hooked fish in the water to keep the school by the boat enabling them to catch more. Dan and Jeff looked at Pete in surprise as he wrapped the leader around his hand and lifted the fish out of the water. It flapped across the deck, scattering blood everywhere, before he finally got it into the box.

"Hey," Jeff said. "What about the rest."

"Later. We need to talk," Pete said as they gathered in the shade provided by the T-top over the center console.

"What the fuck do you think you were doing with that little party last night? Now your wives know. What's next, take it home and have a block party?"

Their heads hung low. "Take it easy. We only told them we found one brick. They don't know anything more than that."

Pete decided to allow them their secret of the missing bricks. "Okay, well, I got sick of your little orgy, so I went out. Met this guy that can help us."

"So, you just met some guy, told him everything, and you're pissed at us? Did he come with a resume?"

"It's not like that." Pete explained the Key West trip.

Dan slapped Pete on the back and Jeff fist bumped him. "Way to go, son. Didn't think you had it in you."

Pete blushed. "Anyway, I saw this guy go out and score some stuff." He turned on them. "Look, we've got to get rid of this stuff, do it ourselves or trust someone. After what you guys did last night, if this stuff finds its way to Tampa, we'll be on the front page of the paper - either in handcuffs or dead in a gutter."

"So, what do you have in mind?"

"When I described the packages and told him about the initials, he thought he might know the guy. Said maybe we could get a finder's fee for returning it." He paused, "Look, it's found money. You saw that guy in the boat point his finger like a gun at us yesterday. These guys won't think twice about killing us to get their stuff back." He waited to see their reaction before continuing. "How do you think you're going to sell it off without getting caught. Just because it's worth a crap load of money at street value doesn't mean we can sell it."

"A score like that and we just get a finders fee?" Jeff asked.

"And we cut him in for brokering it."

"And split it. I don't know about that. This could pay off my plastic and house if I play it right. Hell, I could retire on this," Jeff said.

"You guys really think we're capable of selling this stuff without getting in trouble? We don't even know where to start."

"I know a guy," Dan said.

"Of course you know a guy. And he knows a guy, and pretty soon all the other guys know about this and we're on the front page and can't even read it because we're wearing cement boots having crabs bite our balls."

They stood there, each making his own calculations.

You've got a point." Jeff wavered. "I guess I'm good if we take this to him, see what he has in mind for a reward."

"I don't know, guys. I could really use a big score," Dan whined. "You guys know what the real estate market has done to me."

"And you're just gonna walk into town and pay everything off? Don't you think the IRS is going to have some questions?"

He put his head down in defeat. "Alright. I'll go along. Looks like I'm outvoted anyway."

* * *

The fly kissed the water, leader following in a loop, and Mac started to strip the line back in. Two quick pulls, one slow pull, rinse and repeat, until he'd recovered the line. He balanced on his paddleboard, paddle resting on the board between his legs, as he restarted the casting motion.

The snook hit the fly as soon as it hit the water, jumped, and made a run for the safety of the mangroves. Mac used the bend of the rod to muscle him out into the open, then quickly reeled the slack line in and started pumping the fish toward his board. Minutes later, on his knees, he reached into the water and released the fish. He watched it swim away and thought again how lucky he was to live here. Every month brought something different for him. A retired commercial diver, he lobstered in season and took on whatever salvage jobs came his way. This allowed plenty of time to paddle and fish.

The tide was easing now, working toward the slack period where the water had no current, so he stretched the line, hooking the fly to the eyelet near the handle, and switched the rod for the paddle. Slack tide was the least productive for fishing. Moving water brought bait in and out of the flats attracting the larger fish that preyed on it. He started paddling slowly, coasting by the mangroves. He picked up speed as his muscles warmed and he headed into the main channel. The wind on his back and no tidal pull, it was an easy paddle home.

Once there, he lifted the board fin-first over the seawall and carried it to his rack. He'd chosen the touring board today — not as fast, but more stable than his fourteen-inch racing board.

He let himself inside, and noticed the phone vibrating on the counter. Generally averse to electronics, except for GPS and depth finders, he picked up the smartphone. Alerts crowded the screen.

His heart picked up when he read the texts and pecked out YES with his index finger — close to the limit of his texting skills. A quick shower later and he was in his '82 Chevy truck headed south on US1.

The drive to Key West was quiet, most of the traffic moving north as people pulled their boats back to their driveways, vacations over. He eased off the gas again. Anxious to get there he knew better than to speed. Mel was on his mind in a good way as he drove over the Stock Island bridge, entering Key West. He turned left and followed the bend around to the airport.

The tarmac was dotted with small planes. Although *international* was in the title, Key West International was a small field. He noticed his heart rate pick up as he saw her, standing impatiently next to a line of pink cabs. He moved into the right lane and stopped behind the last cab in line.

She got into the cab of his truck. He leaned over for the expected kiss, but instead she smacked him on the arm.

"I was just about to rent a car or take a cab." She pointed at the line up in front of them. "You got that phone, now learn to use it!"

"Sorry, babe." He pulled out from the curb. "I was fishing. Phones aren't much use out there."

"Figures." She pecked him on his cheek and closed the space, moving into the center of the bench seat. "Now turn on the AC."

Chapter 7

Pete wasn't ready to head in yet. He had too much to think about. The highlight reel from the night before was interrupted by the image of the guy in the cigarette boat. Trolling the Gulf Stream steadied him. He looked back, checking the lines and glancing at Dan and Jeff. They had crashed in opposite corners of the boat, looking like Bobblrhead dolls, their heads bouncing with the rhythm of the waves. Pete was deep in thought when the line snapped from the outrigger clip.

The fish splashed twice, way back in the spread. "Get up, guys, it's big," he snapped at his friends.

Dan and Jeff lay unmoving -- more like unconscious. Pete slowed the boat, allowing only enough speed to maintain course. With one eye on the compass, he quickly reeled in the short rods and the line on the port side outrigger. He pulled the last rod out of the holder and pulled back on the fish. It jumped again and sounded. One hand on the rod and the other on the wheel, he adjusted course and set the boat in neutral. He'd have preferred someone to drive, so he could chase the fish, but that wasn't happening.

He pumped the rod, slowly bringing the fish to the boat, then let it run when it needed. Sweaty fingers tightening the drag slightly, hoping the additional tension on the line would wear the fish out faster. He saw it for the first time as it swung, holding in the current like a flag. The hot blue was fading to green on its back, signaling that it was almost spent. One more run and Pete had him at the boat again. He eased the drag, set the rod in the holder, and grabbed the gaff. The fish was swimming with the boat now, both moving with the current. He gently wrapped the leader around his hand, guiding the fish closer while he set the gaff in the water. He pulled the gaff up, moving backward into the boat as he lifted.

Dan's outstretched leg caught him and sent him to the deck. A small fish could wreak havoc in a boat. A thirty-pound bull like this could do some serious damage. Pete regained his footing and grabbed the gaff while the fish slapped at the bodies, startling them awake. He moved towards the bow, kicking open the large fish box with his foot. One final swing and the fish was in the box. Pete was spent, but all grins as he pulled the gaff out and closed the cover. He left the lure in the fish, leader sticking out of the box, waiting for it to quiet before he extracted the hook. He sat on the cooler and thought about the hot streak he was on.

It wasn't going to get any better than this, he thought as he stowed the gear and headed towards the Sombrero Light House which marked the reef. As they crossed the reef line the water turned glassy calm allowing him to push the boat to the limit. They were all awake as they cruised into the channel toward their rental house. It was dead quiet when they pulled up, no sign of the girls. Pete docked the boat and jumped onto the old wood.

"I won't tell your wives what worthless pieces of crap you were out there today if you get off your butts and clean the boat and fish. I've got business to take care of."

He headed to the house with a swagger in his step. The living room remained in disarray, absent of bodies. He grabbed a beer from the refrigerator and dialed Trufante's number.

"Hey, man, talked to my buddies and they're in."

"Good call. I'll call the dude and see what I can set up. I need to see the stuff so I can tell him what you've got. I'm sure it's his, just want to cover my bases."

Pete gave him the address. "How long?"

"Finish my beer and I'll head on over."

Pete sat at the counter, reality closing in on him. The euphoria of catching the fish was gone, Joanie forgotten, as he thought about the exchange that was going to happen. He was an insurance guy ... risk averse. Exchanging a pile of coke with a drug dealer was not in his wheelhouse.

* * *

Fifteen minutes later, Pete heard the roar of pipes as a motorcycle pulled in the driveway. He looked out the sliding glass door, checking that Dan and Jeff were still occupied with the boat; it looked like they were doing more drinking than cleaning, but they weren't going anywhere. He had lost all the swagger from earlier as he went out to meet Trufante. They met in the driveway.

"Where's it at?"

"Come on. It's in the storeroom." Pete led the way.

As they rounded the corner, Trufante saw the two men cleaning the boat. "They know to stay away, right dude. They don't need to know who I am or what I look like." He flashed the grin. "And I tend to stand out in a crowd."

"Yeah, they're good." Heat poured from the room as Pete opened the door.

"Man, you need some air in here." They were in the storage room, door closed.

They were both dripping sweat as they moved the gear, uncovering the cooler. Pete opened the lid and took out a brick.

"Here you go. Had fifty, but my worthless buddies took one each. There's forty-seven now. One was different. I took it out. Don't know what it is — wrapped the same, but in some kind of metal box."

"If it was part of the bundle, I need that one too."

"All right - I'll be right back. Pete thought about hopping in his car and going home. Trufante knew where the drugs were, he could extricate himself from the whole deal right now. Dan and

Jeff would land on their feet ... they always did. But he was still cocky from the fish and Joanie. He returned a few minutes later and handed the brick to Trufante.

Trufante examined it carefully. "Don't know what this is, but if it's part of the bundle he's going to want it back."

"I don't mind handing over drugs, but there's something not right about this. I have a bad feeling about what this could be."

"I'm a little curious myself. Here, crack 'er open, let's have a look." He handed the box back to Pete.

Pete removed the wrapper, exposing the dull sheen of lead. It had curved corners and a solder joint where the top attached. He ran his hand around the soldered seal. "Any ideas?"

Trufante took the box back and turned it in his hands. "Now you've got my attention. I got a buddy could probably open it. Maybe know what it is by looking at it."

"What about the rest of the deal?"

"Let's see what this is all about first." He shook the box causing Pete to jump. "Maybe raise the stakes some. I'll call the dude when I get back."

They walked from the room and closed the door, both noticing the drop in temperature once in the shade of the carport. Trufante glanced towards the dock. "No reason to tell your buddies about this."

* * *

Al Green swooned Mac and Mel into a slow dance as they cooked dinner. Fresh snapper, barbecued with olive oil and oregano, with a side of jasmine Thai rice and some steamed veggies. They liked to keep it simple. A half-full bottle of white wine sat on the counter with a shared glass. The music and chemistry was moving them toward the bedroom when Mac's phone rang.

He glanced at the display and grabbed the phone. "It's Tru. You mind? I want to see if he wants to fish with me tomorrow."

He pressed the accept button. "Hey."

"Got something you ought to see."

"Bring it by in the morning and I'll have a look, then we can head out. I heard the stream's running close and there are some big fish out there. Come by at six."

"Rather do it now."

"No way," he glanced at Mel's backside as she went towards the bedroom. "Be here at six."

"You got the coffee, I'll be there."

The mood was only broken for a moment, and then the bedroom door closed behind them.

Chapter 8

Trufante stepped off the motorcycle. The palm fronds barely rustled. The light breeze would make for smooth seas, but would also make it hotter than ten Hells. Daylight barely illuminated the path to the house as Trufante navigated it and let himself in. Mac's house was the last building on a street of mostly manufactured homes. Each house had a postage-stamp lot covered in gravel, outlined by low cinder block walls, the decade of construction evident by the design of the wall and siding on the house. In most communities it would be just another trailer park in the middle of a city, but here each lot had a section of seawall, the boats docked there worth more than the houses.

Mac's house was a two-story structure which towered over the adjacent manufactured homes. The exterior was clad in metal. The corrugated siding and roof showed a little rust, but was mostly indestructible, even in this climate. Inside the downstairs was set aside as a workshop and storage area, the upstairs the living quarters. An atrium added on later gave the house a unique look, separating it from the standard Keys' stilt houses. The addition, built out toward the street, enclosed the old exterior staircase and upstairs balcony.

Mac and Mel were in the kitchen sharing coffee, both dressed for work. Mel had on an Armani business suit and heels. Mac was wearing shorts and a T-shirt.

"Damn, girl, looking good," Trufante said as he went for the coffee.

"Got a court hearing in Key West this morning." She got up and hugged Mac, ending the embrace with a kiss. Trufante got a smack on the shoulder as she grabbed her briefcase and Mac's keys. "Sure you don't need this?"

"No, we'll be on the water all day. Good luck. Text me later. We'll be out of range most of the day."

"Text me later," she mimicked him. She turned towards Trufante. "Six months ago he didn't know what a text message was, now look at him."

Mac ignored the jibe and they both watched her go. He turned toward Tru. "What do you want me to look at?"

He watched as Trufante reached into his pack and pulled out a paper bag from which he extracted the box. Mac reached for it.

"Let's take this down and have a look. Lead cased - how'd you come across this anyway?" He was reluctant to even ask the question, but he had to know. Trufante had a habit of stepping in trouble every time he walked out the door. A lead box was not a good sign. Once downstairs they moved over to a large wooden workbench. Gear and tools were spread across it. Mac cleared a space near a large vise clamped to the counter. He moved a magnified light over and looked at it. "The lids soldered on too. How 'bout that story?"

"Just met some dude come across it. Told him I knew someone that might know what it is."

Mac knew him better than to accept this as the truth. "Come on, where the hell did it come from?"

As Mac listened to the story he set the box down and placed a rag around it. Once wrapped he set it in the jaws of the vise and tightened it carefully. The rag prevented the vise from leaving any marks on the box. He wasn't sure he wanted anyone to know it had been examined.

Trufante finished the story. "I don't mind brokering the return of the drugs, but this? Looks like someone's trying to hide something with this setup." He pointed to the box.

"Let's have a look." Mac moved the magnifying light over

the vise. He took a drill with a 1/16-inch bit and bored a tiny hole into the solder line. This would allow him a chance to cover his tracks by soldering the hole and then polishing it to match the existing solder. He reversed the drill and extracted the bit. Carefully, he removed the box from the vise and tapped it, drilled corner down on the workbench. A thin pile of material started to accumulate. He turned the box over and set it aside.

"Powder, pretty fine and yellow." He set the box on the table and pulled a ladder over to some shelves. The shelves were packed with boxes, many housing tools from his days as a commercial diver. He searched for several minutes, muttering under his breath about what a mess this place was. Finally, buried behind several boxes he found what he was looking for and set the metal case on the bench. The geiger counter was an older model, but still functional.

"What the hell are you doing with one of those?"

"There's quite a bit of radioactive stuff in compaction testing equipment. We used to use a lot of it back in the day. It was all in small quantities, but you still want to make sure that you're not exposed when you're working on something."

He took the wand from the counter and held it over the pile. The meter jumped into the red zone, indicating radioactivity. "There's your answer. I hoped I never saw another grain of this after we dumped those bombs."

"You know how potent it is?"

"I can run some tests, but my guess, the way the meter went right to red with this tiny sample, is it's plutonium 239."

"That's not good is it?"

"Nope. Means this has pretty much got to be terrorists. Crap." Mac took the drill bit and rinsed it thoroughly in the sink. He let the water run for several minutes, then bagged the drill bit, wrapped it in a baggie, and tossed it in the trash. "Get the boat going. I'll solder this hole. We can figure out what to do with this while we're out there. How hot is this anyway?" he asked, hoping

Trufante hadn't done anything to implicate him in his latest mess.

"Haven't gone to anyone yet. Just the dudes that found it and you." He walked out towards the boat.

Mac soldered the hole and took the brick to his office — a small space off the workshop. He placed it on his desk, then removed the foul weather gear that hid the safe. He keyed in the combination, opened the safe, and placed the box on a shelf next to his revolver. He needed to think about what to do here. He could go to the authorities, but how would he explain how he got it without implicating himself and Trufante. No harm in a couple of hours out on the water, got some bills to pay anyway, he thought. He closed the safe and headed to the boat.

Chapter 9

Mel walked into the courtroom with practiced ease. She'd been appearing, often on her own, in federal courts like this for eight years now, and knew exactly what to expect. She would have a team of lawyers and paralegals if this were the actual trial, but she often handled motion hearings alone. Davies and Associates cases tended to be complicated, with many motions clogging the stream of justice. Judges hated these cases, many destined for several appeals, and eventually the Supreme Court. Every move they made, every motion they ruled on, would have another judge or panel of judges looking over their shoulders as the appeals rose through the court system.

In this case, the ACLU was tied in as well. Liberal and conservative groups had both been sparring with the government over the use of drones on US soil for the past several years. This case might be the one that brought it all to bear. But Mel swore this was the last cause she would fight for the advocacy group. Some of their causes were strict constitutional issues, like drone use, but others had a very political agenda. Cases were often selected for who they represented rather than the constitutional issue. Through law school and the years after she had often doubted the relevance of the Constitution, often claiming that it was outdated and didn't apply to the real world. Now her views were diverging from that. If she looked in the mirror, she knew she would see some of her dad in her, more strongly represented than she may have liked.

Davies and Associates vs. The United States Navy was the latest in the cases involving the use of drones. Mel had a direct interest in this case, as both attorney and witness. Now-retired

Naval captain, James Gillum, sat at the opposite table, with several uniformed JAG attorneys to represent him. Gillum had been directly involved in the drone surveillance of her father's private island. Mel had witnessed this firsthand and seen the deception of the captain.

This motion, presented by the Navy, was an attempt to deny her the ability to be council and witness on the same case. It was the Navy's plan to force her hand, hoping her ego would choose attorney over witness, which would then weaken the case. What they failed to realize was her resolve and, although she was not ready to admit it, the desire for revenge. This case had led to her father's death, and she was ready to lay that squarely at Jim Gillum's Navy-issue polished shoes.

She went to the prosecutor's table and sat down. Patel was already seated, looking smug, sorting through a file, ignoring her as she moved towards him.

Not wanting a scene, she sat intentionally leaving an empty chair between them. "Remember, I am the lead on this?" she whispered through clenched teeth.

"We'll see about that," he responded.

The hearing was informal — the judge entered without fanfare, no bailiff or robes. He crossed the polished floor and sat at the bench, nodding to the court reporter to begin transcribing the session. He checked his watch, obviously already counting down the minutes until lunch, then looked over to the crowded defense table.

"You have a motion to dismiss Ms. Woodson as council for this case."

"Yes, sir," the uniformed attorney responded. "We see it as a clear conflict of interests to have Ms. Woodson as council and lead witness. "

"What do you base this on?"

The attorney glanced at his legal pad and read off a

43

precedent. "It's clear in rule 3.7 of the American Bar Association that a lawyer can't testify in her own case. There are several exemptions," he paused for effect, "but none apply to this case."

"Ms. Woodson, your response?"

Mel sat straight in her chair. "Your Honor, I am an eyewitness to this incident. You could say that I am representing myself. There's nothing wrong with that, to my knowledge."

The judge looked toward the defense table, waiting for an answer.

"Sir, this is not simply a matter of self representation. Ms. Woodson is council for the plaintiff in this case, not for herself. She is therefore representing Davies and Associates, not herself. In addition, as a witness, we intend to call her to testify at trial. Once she takes that role, she is no longer in a position to protect her client. It is a clear conflict of interests."

The argument raged back and forth for several more rounds. Mel knew she was on shaky ground to start, but sometimes you had to role the dice. The truth, if she would admit it to herself, was that she was too emotionally vested in the case to make an impartial decision like this. What was best for the case and what would satisfy her desire for revenge were not the same. She was running out of steam and glanced over at Patel for any input. He was doodling on his pad, not even engaged in the discussion. It would become his case if she were asked to step down. She sensed the judge losing interest. She had her fears confirmed when he ruled.

"Ms. Woodson, this is a procedural issue. There is a very strong possibility that this case will be appealed. In fact, I'd call it a certainty. And this issue is going to be brought up at every level. I don't want to waste the taxpayers' money and conduct an expensive trial, just to have it deemed a mistrial on appeal. You will have to step down as lead council if you insist on being a material witness. You may assist with the case, but not in your current role."

She fidgeted in her chair. There was never any doubt the judge would do the safe thing and the decision was what she'd expected. If Mac would have agreed to testify, she could have played this differently. Why he refused would be a topic for later. She'd left it alone until now, knowing he had a reason, but now it affected her and her case. She called the Navy's bluff. She was sure they had counted on her recessing herself as a witness. "I will step down as lead attorney and assist on the case, in order to remain a witness." She said it grudgingly, not wanting to give up the power, but realized that it was the best she could do. She'd just have to watch Patel's every move.

At least she'd still be a witness on the trial. The Navy wasn't going to keep her from doing *that*.

"If that is all then...." The judge looked at each table, waiting for a nod in the affirmative.

"Actually, your Honor, there is a matter I would like to submit to you," Patel said.

The Navy council rose. "There is nothing else slated for today."

"Sit down, this is an informal hearing." The judge turned to Patel, "Mr. Patel, I will allow you to present your motion, but cannot guarantee we will hear it."

"Thank you. Just a matter of discovery. We would like to have access to the surveillance logs the Navy has on Ms. Woodson and Mac Travis. Phone records, emails, texts."

The judge motioned for a response.

"The Navy does not perform data collection," the JAG said with no reaction.

"Oh, so you don't perform surveillance of Americans on American soil. Really?" Patel checked his notes and continued. "Your computers are tied to the NSA. They have the data, and we want it."

The judge pondered the motion, then faced the defense table.

"If it's on your computers and relates to this case, they can have it." He looked at both tables. "If that is all…."

* * *

Mel was steaming as she followed a smug Patel out of the courtroom. "What the hell was that?"

"What? I'm lead on this case now. That evidence is important."

"This is about drones, not electronic surveillance. You can't have it all." She saw his motives. The drones were directly tied to her father's death. Wood had revealed the truth about a coverup of two nuclear bombs jettisoned during the Cuban Missile Crisis. The vice president and Gillum were directly involved in both the original incident and the coverup. Gillum had then illegally used a Navy drone to spy on her dad's island. Mac had been there with her and had seen it. Now Patel was trying to use the national attention the case was assured by the vice president's involvement for his own agenda.

"Really. We can win on both counts, you know. I don't give a crap about your dad and the Navy sending a drone to find a bomb that was actually *there*. Sure is a great story, though, and will attract the media in droves."

Mel growled. "So, you're setting me up. Using my dad's death as an excuse to get what you want. Using all of this as a way to get the government to admit that they're tracking us."

He shrugged. "You shouldn't even be associated with this case, except as a witness. I'll have to talk to Davies about putting a leash on you. Not like you get a say in how I run the case. And I'm not so sure how well your bitch mode is going to look to a jury."

"I'll show you bitch mode. Watch your back. This bitch is after you."

He ignored the threat, "I'm on a plane back to DC tonight. Stay out of trouble," he warned.

Chapter 10

Trufante slipped the knife into the fish, skillfully making a small incision around the area the filet would come from, adjusting the blades course to navigate the knuckles on the spine. The filet came off cleanly, leaving a translucent skeleton remaining. The carcass went into the barrel next to him, to be ground for chum, as he moved onto the next fish.

The pile was getting smaller as the sun descended, and the mosquitos joined the black flies. Trufante sipped from his beer and picked up the pace. Mac was cleaning the boat while he cleaned the fish. He knew Mac would soon finish and help, cutting his remaining work load in half. Most days he would be more focused on drinking beer than cleaning fish, but not today. He was anxious to get on the phone and make some money, so he swatted flies and kept going. Pete had left him several anxious messages and he smelled a payoff on the horizon.

He whipped through the remaining fish and added them to the cooler at his feet, then washed the cleaning table and knife, and finally de-slimed his hands. The sound of a fresh beer cracking indicated that his work day was over. He grabbed his phone and went toward the table and chairs outside the house. He checked that Mac was still on the boat. Out of hearing range, he dialed the number from memory. Not a good idea to have a drug dealer's phone number in your contact list.

"Cesar, you missing something?"

"That you, Cajun? What you talkin' about?"

"Maybe somebody picked something up in the stream the

other day. Maybe it's yours." Trufante dangled the bait.

"I'll play along with your game. Supposing I did lose something, and supposing you know where it is, what would you want to return it to its rightful owner?"

"It's not me, man. If I had it, I'd run it right down there and trust your benevolence." He sipped his beer, letting the tension build.

"Come on. Let's have it or I'll come up there and force it out of you."

Trufante set the hook, "See, I ran into this dude in a bar, told me a story. Checked it out and it's legit. Believe it … fools think they can piece it out and get rich. Told the dudes you would take care of them for returning it."

"Absolutely," he lied. "Where can I meet these guys?"

"You got an offer I can take to them? There's one that wants to take the stuff and sell it piecemeal. I don't know how easy they'll roll over."

"Ten large do it?"

"I'm thinking not. They know what the stuff is worth. And like I said, there's one dude that is going to be a hard sell." Trufante paused waiting for this to set in. Sure they had decided to go with his plan, but Cesar didn't know that.

"Fifty then. Tell those motherfuckers if they try and sell that stuff anywhere in this state, I'll find them and the consequences will not be pretty. Understand?"

"Hey, man, I'm trying to help you out here, no need to go off on me."

"I appreciate that, and I will not forget your efforts. Take the offer to them and let me know. I've got some guys breathing down my neck to get this back. I'm going to head up there. Let's do this tonight."

* * *

Mac walked up the path as Trufante disconnected. "C'mon

inside, I'll settle up with you."

"Good deal, man. I could use a shot of that rum you got, anyway."

"You seem a little shaky." Mac wondered what the phone call was about. "Come on up. I only keep that crap for you." Mac led the way upstairs. He turned on the fans in an attempt to cool the place.

"You know you're the only dude down here without AC."

Mac ignored him and went to the kitchen. He poured two fingers in a glass and handed it to Trufante. "Don't like AC. The fans work okay for me. Three hundred-dollar bills came out of his billfold and were quickly swallowed up by Trufante's eager hand. "Should be more coming. I'll take it to the market in the morning and let you know."

Trufante showed his teeth. "Good deal, man. What about that other thing?"

Mac reached for the bottle of scotch and poured a matching amount for himself. He held his glass up in silent salutation. "I've been thinking about that. He picked up his phone.

"Hold on there. What'd you have in mind?"

"I'm calling Jules. Let the sheriff's office handle this. She can call in whoever she wants."

"Man, put that away. You see...." He drained his glass, "I'm in a situation here. The stuff's not mine. I got this dude comin' up to take it and that box is part of the package. See these dudes ran across a square grouper and...." He paused and held the empty glass towards Mac. "You can't go there. He'll put a freakin ice pick through me or something."

Mac looked at him, "That's what the secret phone call was about. I knew you were up to something."

"It's a harmless deal, man." Trufante went for the tequila bottle, but Mac knocked his hand away.

"Harmless? You get with some guys that find a square

grouper with some radioactive shit mixed in and it's harmless?"

"Just trying to make a buck. Guess I jumped the gun."

Mac stared at him until the Cajun blinked and shied away. "No way can that stuff get to where it was intended. Okay?. I say we stash what's in there and refill it with something else. I got a compaction tester that has some radioactive material in it. We can mix that stuff with sand or something and unless these guys really know what they're looking at it'll pass a first inspection. It'll test positive with a geiger counter. Any luck it'll get far enough down the line before they figure out what happened. They won't be able to trace it back to you."

"As long as I can pass it off, I'm good with that."

Mel came through the door then, breathing heavily, her clothes stuck to her, sweat dripping from her hair.

"Set it up. I'll do the package up tonight," Mac whispered as he watched Mel climbing the stairs. "Not a word to her," he said as the door opened.

"You're one crazy lady, running in this heat. It's hotter than nine Hells out there," Trufante said.

"Thanks for your concern." She went for the refrigerator and grabbed a beer.

"Hey, babe, maybe grab some water first."

She gave Mac the famous Melanie Woodson FU look, and finished the beer like a college kid on spring break. Then she crushed the can and tossed it in the trash."Pour me some of that," she said, motioning toward the scotch.

"Easy, girl. You're gonna hurt yourself. Guess the hearing didn't go well."

"The Davies and the ACLU set me up, that's all. I'm so done with them. If I could just get justice for dad, I'd quit right now."

Mac had been waiting for these words for a long time. He felt her frustration, but there was more than that at play. He wouldn't admit it, but he was jealous. She was gone all the time.

He knew they had no agreement; both had ducked from that curveball. She still lived in DC and traveled constantly, wherever her cases took her. Knowing how the alcohol would affect her, he poured a small shot.

She drank the shot and pushed the glass toward him, clearly not satisfied. Mac held the bottle and debated his options. He'd seen her drunk once before, after they'd scattered Wood's ashes over his island. It wasn't pretty, and he didn't want to go there again. He put a flat hand over the glass. "I'll have another waiting for you, but please drink some water and take a shower."

Just for spite, she grabbed the bottle and took a shot directly from it. "Fine." She stormed off toward the bedroom, turning before she was out of sight. "And, we're going to have a little chat about why you won't help me out as a witness."

"Got your hands full there, bud," Trufante said as he finished his drink and left.

Chapter 11

"My buddies ... they want to meet you," Pete hesitated anticipating the reaction. He paced the patio outside of the rental house. Every time he passed the glass door he saw Jeff and Dan sitting at the bar watching him.

"No freaking way. I got my neck stuck out too far on this already. This dude we're dealing with is a little south of stable," Trufante said.

"I don't know if I can get them to go along without some assurances. We're pretty much trusting you. I don't even know you. You have to believe they're skeptical."

"Listen, dude, this isn't a bake sale. I'm trying to save your asses here. We've gone past the point of no return just telling him it's found, and now he's on his way to Marathon. It's a small town ... he'll find you."

Pete put the phone down, an uneasy look on his face. He thought about the guy pulling the trigger on the imaginary gun. "He won't meet you. Says he's too involved already."

"I'd like to be too involved, and collect $12,500 for a few phone calls. That's all he's doing," Jeff said.

"Yeah, I still say we keep it and sell it over time. No way he knows," Dan said.

"After seeing your little party the other night, I vote no on that one. It's not going to end well. Remember *Scarface* — the first rule is *not* to use your own stuff. You've already violated that one," Pete said.

Dan stood up, looking like he was going to get aggressive.

"Enough. Pete, go make the exchange, we'll wait here," Jeff

said.

Dan was in Pete's face now. "You pushed this on us. I've reconsidered. You guys return your share. I'll take mine and do what I want with it."

"Sit down," Jeff starred at Dan, "Time for some tough love. Pete's right. Selling drugs is not in your wheelhouse. You'll end up taking us down with you. It's not a ton of money, but it's something and we can wash our hands of this thing."

Dan sat down. They took his silence for acceptance.

* * *

Pete waited for Trufante outside the bar where they first met, the cooler loaded in his trunk. He'd taken a few extra minutes to restock the bricks in the cooler trying to make forty-seven bricks look like fifty. With any luck the guy would just glance at the cooler and not count every brick. Trufante pulled up on his motorcycle and parked next to him. Without a word, he opened the passenger door and got in.

"Howdy, partner. We ready to go get us a payoff?"

"A little nervous. What if he counts them."

"Just gotta keep a poker face."

"Yeah sure," Pete said reluctantly. "Let's go."

"No worries, man, we pull this off and go back to Sue's. Joanie's hanging with her, says she'd like to see you again."

Pete's worry lines eased slightly. "Okay, what do we have to do?"

"All you've got to do is drive, pop the trunk, and look down. Don't get out of the car. Don't look at the dude."

He started the car and backed out of the parking spot. "Where to?"

"Monster Bait. Turn right out of here and go about two hundred yards, take a left. You'll see the place on the left."

Pete drove in silence, apprehensive about the exchange. This was not just a little out of his comfort zone; as an insurance man, it was a *lot* out of his comfort zone. They drove in an uneasy silence. Pete tried to concentrate on the road as Trufante rattled on about their day fishing. They turned into the lot, crab and lobster traps stacked on both sides of the drive.

"How do we know where he is?"

"He'll let us know. Pull up here and hang tight."

Pete felt like he was being watched. He fidgeted while Trufante sat calmly, still messing with the radio, like he'd done this a hundred times before. A few minutes later, a truck's lights flashed three times from a pile of traps about a hundred yards down. Pete looked over at Trufante, who nodded, and pulled the car forward slowly, stopping when he saw the truck, its lights illuminating the scene. The truck was lifted with meaty tires, polished chrome sparkled and neon lit the floorboards. A fluorescent ballyhoo was stenciled on the side with Monster Bait's logo underneath.

"Remember, just stay here and keep your head down. Pop the trunk."

Pete popped the trunk lid and sat quietly while Trufante extricated his large frame from the car and strode over to the truck. The two men talked for a few minutes and Trufante headed back to the car, giving a discreet thumbs up as he approached. Then the trunk lid lifted and he extracted the cooler, his long arms easily reaching both handles.

As Trufante approached the truck, two men emerged from the trap piles on either side, AK-47s pointed at Trufante.

"Just be cool and set the cooler on the tailgate. Nobody needs to get hurt," Pete heard them say through the open window.

"Thought we had a deal, man. What's with the munitions? This ain't cool."

"Do it."

Pete watched, his eyes large and unblinking as Trufante set the package down and stood uneasily as the leader removed and counted the packages. His stomach rolled and he felt sick.

"Forty-seven. Motherfucker, you're short three."

"It ain't on me. Look, Cesar, like I told you, I'm helping you out here. Ask the jerk-off in the car. He's the one that found it."

Pete looked up. Trufante had told him to keep his head down and everything would be alright, but he'd just thrown him under the bus -- and drove over him. Nervously, he jiggled the keys in the ignition thinking about starting the motor and making a run for it.

The gunman glanced at one of the riflemen, communication unspoken, and the guy took off for a nearby shed. A motor started.

"Just the chum machine," Cesar said. "You're a fisherman, you know how it works. Big things go in and little things come out."

Trufante started to back away, hands in the air. "Lemme go talk to the dude." He took a step back towards the car, tripped over a buoy line and landed on the ground. One of Cesar's gunmen was on him instantly, barrel pointed at his chest.

"You're not going anywhere, Cajun. Cover that guy in the car, too," he yelled.

Knowing that he was no longer invisible, Pete looked up and saw the gun pointed at Trufante, still on the ground. His heart stopped beating when he saw the other gun pointed at him. Panic took over and he started the car. But instead of reverse, he stuck it in drive and hit the gas. The car shot forward. The brakes engaged right above Trufante's body, and the gunman jumped to the side. It took a second to react from his mistake, but he was quicker than the gunman. He slammed the car in reverse and floored the gas pedal. The car squealed backwards into a trap pile, causing an avalanche. Some of the higher traps fell on the car, though most of them blocked the road.

Gunshots blazed through the traps — the only obstacle between Pete and the drug runners and he floored the gas pedal again, continuing in reverse, until he hit the main driveway. There he swung back and into forward, tires screeching and shooting the crushed coral surface into the air.

One headlight was shot out, but he didn't think the radiator had been hit. At least he hoped not. He hit the gas pedal again and accelerated out of the fishery's entry, terrified. Behind him, he saw the truck's headlights coming after him.

* * *

Trufante lay on the ground in disbelief. How could easy money go so wrong? The barrel of a pistol looked down at him, Cesar's right eye lined up behind it.

"Get up, you piece of Cajun trash. Let's take a little walk."

Cesar kept the gun pointed at Trufante as he got up, and brushed himself off. He motioned for one of his guys to pick up the package. Then he motioned Trufante toward the shed, the motor getting louder as they approached. As they entered the shed, he caught the glint of gold from the mouth of a very large man, wearing a rubber apron and gloves.

"You got two choices, *amigo*. You go in live or you go in dead. Either way, you're going in. Be feeding yellowtails for fat *touristas* on the reef in a couple of days. Now, tell me a story."

Chapter 12

Mac watched Mel's face as she slept. This was the only time she wasn't full of vigor and passion, and she looked almost angelic. She had showered and fallen immediately into bed, a towel under her still-wet hair. It was the best possible outcome — sleep. She could handle a glass of wine, but sharing his glass was usually enough. Her little binge earlier was way past her threshold, and it had knocked her out cold. He covered her with a light blanket and left the room.

Downstairs in his shop, he went to the workbench and turned on the magnifying light. The box, recovered from the office safe, sat on the table. He stared at it wondering what to do. It would have been too easy to turn it into the authorities. He knew Trufante was a magnet for trouble, either through karma or desire he wasn't sure. In any event, he realized that he was here now and he had to help his friend. His brain swirled with the task ahead. The radioactive material in the box was more than dangerous. If it was what he thought, it could blow Marathon and half the Keys with it. He took a deep breath and took control of his thoughts. His first priority was to make sure the terrorists didn't get the real material.

A welding apron, gloves, and mask protected him as he clamped the box in the vise and drilled a larger hole in the same spot as the pilot hole he'd drilled earlier. He poured the contents onto a plate.

Lead was the preferred medium to protect against radiation. He scrounged around the shop and found a milk crate with an assortment of diving weights, then pulled out a large propane burner he used to cook stone crabs and took them outside. He stood over a large burner, moving an old pan back and forth over the flame, watching as the two sacrificial weights melted into a puddle. Then, the heat adjusted to keep the lead molten, he went back inside, searching for something to make a mold.

A crab buoy caught his eye. Worried that the styrofoam would burn away, however, he tested a small piece. The lead smoked against the styrofoam, but didn't burn it. He sawed the buoy in half and scooped out an area large enough to hold the material, half from each side, then whittled the buoy so there was a half - inch of material around the chamber. That should be enough of a shield to encase the plutonium. Put together, it was now the size of a softball. Back at the bench, he poured the material into the chamber and joined the halves, holding them together with hot glue.

The ball rolled in the pan, slowly turning grey as the lead adhered to it. He rotated the ball until the molten lead was used up and set it aside to cool. Geiger counter in hand, he ran it over the lead encased ball. The needle stayed in the green, indicating that it was safe. That was good enough for now, he thought. Next, he needed to fill the lead box and reseal it.

The space below the bench was full of gear. Mac was on his knees, pulling out tools, wondering why he could keep a boat so organized while his work space was a disaster. The compaction tester was all the way in the back, dusty from the years it had sat there untouched. He hadn't needed the tester since he retired from commercial diving ten years ago. He lifted the compactor onto the bench and started to take it apart. The tester, called a nuclear densitometer lay in pieces. It held a small amount of radioactive material in it to test for soil compaction. The radioactive material removed from the unit, Mac lay the parts of the tester aside. The material from the tester was impotent compared to the brick, perfect for a red herring. A geiger counter reacted to radioactivity.

It didn't specify the type. The material from the tester would cause a reaction. It would take a nuclear engineer to realize it wasn't the more potent plutonium he'd removed.

Relieved, he cleaned up and took the lead ball out to the boat. He'd dispose of it in the morning. He was just placing the box back in the safe when Mel startled him.

"Hey, whatcha doing?"

"Oh, it's nothing."

"My head hurts."

He went up to her, hurrying before she had a chance to come down. "Quite the binge for you. Surprised you're even up."

"Sorry about that. I was so pissed at my boss. I came back and ran the old bridge to Pigeon Key and back. Still pissed."

"Four miles in this heat, and I know you didn't take it slow. Just glad you made it back. Want to talk about it?"

"Not now. I'm cool, don't want to get all worked up again. Tomorrow." She kissed him and headed upstairs.

Still a little shaky from the work, he poured himself another scotch and went out on the back deck. He was in over his head and he knew it. With any luck, Trufante could pass off the bricks without incident. He assumed the material was headed to a terrorist group. Who else would smuggle in plutonium? These groups were seldom highly trained. He hoped they wouldn't notice the less potent material. Whatever they made with it would be harmless. He would hide the lead ball with the real material where no one would find it tomorrow morning.

The phone vibrated on the counter, but he ignored it.

* * *

"Where is the last brick then? I'll deal with the gringos about what they have stolen and snorted."

The man in the apron dragged him closer to the chum grinder. He hit the power switch and the motor whirled.

"Cajun. You going to answer?"

59

STEVEN BECKER

Before he could answer the man grabbed his hand and stuffed it into the inlet. He struggled, but the man was more powerful. His wrist was buried in the intake when the blades found his index finger.

"*Alto.*" Cesar yelled over the noise. The man started pushing harder … then restrained himself. He backed away, allowing Trufante to extricate his hand from the machine. It came out dripping blood. He grabbed for a towel and fell to his knees.

"Well, Cajun, do you have something to say?"

"Shit, I would have told you without this." He held up the mangled hand.

Cesar ignored him. He said something in Spanish to the butcher, who quickly left, flashing a quick smile at Trufante on his way out.

"Well?"

"Give me my phone." Trufante was sweating, dialing with his right hand as blood dripped from his left. He writhed in pain, waiting for Mac to answer, his pinkie finger missing to the knuckle.

"Better find your friend there, or we'll have to go deeper."

"He's not answering. I don't know what's up. I need a freakin' doctor," he whimpered.

"When I have my property back I will dump your sorry Cajun ass at the hospital"

Trufante was desperately trying to save his remaining digits. Torture was *not* in his wheelhouse, and he would have caved in before losing the tip of his finger if the sadistic bastard in the apron hadn't wanted to draw blood so badly. "We can just go over there."

"What about the driver, how do we find him? First we take care of that loose end, then we can go see your friend."

"Yeah, whatever, just get me away from this butcher shop."

* * *

Pete pulled into the parking lot of the bar where he'd met

Trufante the other night, still shaking. He sat in the car, not knowing what to do. The deal had gone south — no money, no drugs, and some serious badasses were after him. He didn't think they'd look for him in a bar, but he had to hide the car. He pulled out and headed around the back of the building, the driveway running parallel with the dock that serviced the charter boats. He carefully selected a space not visible from the road, parked, and headed into the bar.

Chapter 13

Trufante's finger, or what was left of it, throbbed. He'd controlled the bleeding by tying a piece of monofilament fishing line he'd found on the floor of the bait house around it and cinched it tight. A dirty rag was clutched over it, absorbing any wayward blood.

"Don't bleed in the truck, Cajun. I'll make you ride in the back," Cesar snorted from the front seat.

Trufante didn't answer. He had no idea how to get out of this. He'd willingly given up the address where Pete was staying — how else did you deal with these psychos, who cut off body parts first and ask questions later? Besides, Pete had ditched him as fast as he could, saving his own skin, and he figured that meant he had the right to do the same.

They pulled up to the rented house and parked next to the Excursion in the driveway. The house was dark and quiet as they walked up the path. Trufante had begged to stay in the truck, but Cesar opened the door and grabbed his good arm, dragging him towards the house.

"Knock," Cesar ordered as he ducked out of view. Trufante knocked on the door and waited.

"Maybe no one's home."

"The car is here, and it's not the same one as the guy who was with you. That means someone's here, and I'm betting they know where my drugs are." Cesar knocked harder, with the butt of his gun. Still no answer. He signaled one of his men to go around back while he waited in front.

"Back door is open." The guy's voice came from around the corner.

Cesar pushed Trufante in front of him as they made their way around the house. Cool air escaped as the sliding glass door opened. They entered slowly, the two men fanning out, checking the kitchen, bathroom, and garage. They concentrated on the bedrooms next. A closed door appeared on the right, two others on the left. One door was open, the room empty. They moved past the bathroom to the two closed doors.

One swift kick from Cesar's boot left the door hanging on one hinge. Two lumps in the bed shifted, but didn't wake as they entered the room. Trufante stayed behind in the hall.

"That's my shit." Cesar walked over and stuck his finger in the mountain of white powder on the table. He licked his finger, confirming his initial reaction. "These fuckin' gringos are partying on my shit," he screamed.

He went to the bed and stared at the two sleeping bodies. Incensed, he grabbed the mattress and dumped it on the floor. The bodies landed on top of each other. They started to unravel themselves from the sheets when a booted toe landed on each of them.

"Stay where you are." He turned as he heard the other door open. "Jose, take these two into the living room."

"What's going on here?" The man stood in the other doorway a woman's hair visible behind him.

"You enjoying my stuff too?" Cesar snapped. Turning, he pushed the newcomers into the living room as well.

* * *

Trufante took one of the chairs. The two couples huddled together on the couch, obviously terrified. The women were weeping, the men wide eyed in disbelief. Cesar and his drug runner stood over them, freely waving their guns around.

"I want my shit back and you will pay for what is missing," Cesar started.

"*We* found it, and who says it's yours? We don't owe you

anything," Dan said.

Cesar went up to him and placed the gun to his forehead. He pulled the trigger without warning, and blood and brain matter sprayed over the living room. Trufante looked on, the pain forgotten. Somehow he needed to get out of here and warn Mac.

The women were screaming now, inching away from the body.

"Whatever you want. Just don't hurt us. I'll get it for you," Jeff said, starting to rise.

"Now, that's the kind of attitude I like to see. Sit right there. Jose will get it. Tell him where it is."

Jose went towards the bedrooms. He came back with two opened bricks, each with about a quarter missing. He started toward the kitchen, ostensibly looking for a plate to scrape up what was scattered around the house, but Cesar stopped him.

Trufante watched in horror. He'd been around commercial fishermen for long enough to know that his finger would heal. But, killing the dude was way out there. "They didn't take much. Why don't you take it off their finders fee?" He pleaded.

"Ain't no finders fee now. They'll pay for all that. Don't worry about it." He turned back to the people in front of him. "Looks like you owe me a half a brick. That'll be a hundred large."

"I don't have a hundred grand." Jeff put his hands out in front of him, pleading for understanding.

Cesar shrugged, unperturbed. "That's including my good customer discount. You have twenty-four hours to come up with it. I'll take the women as collateral."

"Don't let him do this!" one of the women screamed.

Jeff moved to comfort her. "Donna, babe, It's going to be okay. I'll get what they want. You guys just keep cool." He turned to Cesar. "Okay, but I need to go to Tampa and back. I need some more time."

"Drive fast, gringo."

Cesar motioned the women off the couch. They rose as one, clutching each other, and he nodded at Trufante, who rose as well. They looked like a funeral procession walking single-file to the truck.

* * *

Pete looked around the bar. It was about half-full — quieter than the night before. He scanned the crowd for Joanie and Sue, but didn't see them. Hoping they were regulars, he sat at the bar and waited for the bartender to make her way to him. He needed someone to talk to. His mind spun with the possibilities of what was going on now. What had they done to Trufante? What about Dan, Jeff, and the girls? He reached for his phone and dialed Jeff's number. It went to voicemail. He texted a message for him to call.

"What can I get you, hon?"

"I'm trying to find a couple of girls that were here last night. Sue and Joanie."

"Aren't we all." She winked at him.

"Maybe you remember the guy I was talking to. Tall, thin, lots of teeth."

"Oh, that's Tru. I can't give out any numbers, but I'll call him for you."

"I'm actually looking for Joanie. We kind of hit it off," he said, knowing Trufante was in no position to answer his phone.

"Don't have her number, but I know she works over at Fisherman's Hospital. Why don't you check over there?"

"Thanks. I will. How 'bout a shot of Jack. Hell, make it a double." Pete badly needed something to calm him down.

She set the shot glass in front of him. It barely hit the bar top before he slammed the shot. He got up and left a ten on the bar.

Back outside, he sat in his car and dialed. He took a chance and dialed Trufante's number first which went straight to voicemail, and he hung up without leaving a message. Whatever had happened to the guy, he didn't need some stranger listening to a voicemail that might implicate him in the wrongdoing. He pulled out of the lot and drove aimlessly towards US1. With no plan, he sat an extra minute at the stop sign deciding which way to go when he saw the black truck with the neon floorboards and ballyhoo stenciled on its sides. Steeled by the bourbon and not knowing what else to do, he backed out of the lot and followed.

The truck was heading south, toward Key West. He tried to stay several cars back, but got nervous about losing them and crept closer. He was right behind them at the red light, his one working headlight revealing what looked like three heads in the backseat. It looked like one tall guy — possibly Trufante — and two women.

The truck turned left on FifteenthStreet. Halfway down the street, the driver cut the lights. Pete felt vulnerable now, and found a house with no cars in the driveway, where he could hide the car. He got out and followed on foot.

Chapter 14

Mac jumped out of bed. He'd just dozed off when the sound of the front door being kicked in woke him. His first instinct was to grab Mel and get out. The extra hundred and ten pounds didn't slow him as he went out the sliding door onto the deck and headed down the stairs. They were at the dock when she came to, eyes wide and started to open her mouth. Mac put a finger to his lips. Just as he set her down, the lights went on in the house. Mel went over the gunwale first and Mac followed wondering what kind of trouble Trufante had gotten him into now. This had to have something to do with the plutonium.

They went into the cabin, and Mel sat on a bunk, naked. "What the hell's going on?"

Mac ignored her as he peered through the window. Seeing nothing but lights, he went for the revolver hidden behind an access panel in the main stateroom. Back on deck, he screened himself behind the winch and watched. Mel crept up behind him wrapped in a towel.

* * *

Trufante was the last in the house, nudged through the door by the barrel of Cesar's hitman's gun. The initial shock of the mauling had worn off, but his finger still throbbed incessantly. He was trying not to think about the fact that he'd have to live the rest of his life with only half a finger -- if he lived at all.

The two women in front of him were still sobbing hysterically. There was nothing he could do to comfort them with a gun in his back.

"Jose, stay down here with the gringos. I'm going to have a look upstairs." He disappeared up the staircase, returning seconds later. "He's gone. Cajun, I swear to Mary that I will take all your fingers off and feed them to the fish if you warned him."

"What are you talking about? I've been with you the whole time. You've got my phone."

Cesar moved towards Trufante, took his hand and pinched the stub. Trufante's eyes bugged out from the pain. "I'm watching you. Where is the last package?"

Trufante stumbled as he went towards the workbench. He'd already noticed the box missing, but had no alternative than to go through the process. Cesar followed him to the spot where Mac had examined the box. "It was here the last I saw of it." Cesar reached for his finger again, but Trufante saw him coming and jerked it back. "Let's check the office, that's where he would have put it." He was running out of options.

Trufante used his good hand to sort through the desk and shelves. Cesar stood in the door, watching. "Hurry up, Cajun."

"Give me a minute, there's a ton of crap in here." He moved toward the closet with the gun safe, and hid his surprise at finding the door open. Placing his body to block Cesar's view, he grasped a gun. He could take down Cesar, but the other guy was outside, and would be on him as soon as he fired. He needed to work his way toward the back door before he shot, leaving himself an exit route.

"Move, Cajun," Cesar barked. He'd obviously seen the safe, then, and guessed at what it might contain.

Trufante let the towel in his hand fall loosely over the gun as he moved backwards, watching as Cesar couldn't resist the lure of the safe. He went right for it and started searching the shelves as Trufante backed out of the room. He went towards the girls, who were huddled together and tried to move them slowly towards the rear door. Jose was staring at the office waiting for Cesar to appear as they started inching their way out. He eyed the office door hoping for a few extra seconds to get out and make their escape.

"Got it!" Cesar yelled. He came out of the office with the brick-shaped box. He looked at the girls standing by the rear door. "Jose, we don't need them anymore."

"Now?" Jose asked.

Cesar nodded in the affirmative, and Jose shot them, execution style. They fell to the ground, still clutching each other. Trufante had to make his move now. He raised the gun, his hand shaking violently from the pain. The first shot got Jose in the leg, putting him on the floor. He whirled, looking for Cesar, and saw that the man had hidden behind one of the columns. Trufante took a shot at him, knowing it would miss, but hoping to gain enough time to make it out the door. He glanced at the blood pooling around the bodies on the concrete floor. Nothing he could do now - he had to move.

As he dove through the door, both Mexicans fired, their bullets dinging the door jamb on either side of him. He rolled and shot back twice, then heard another shot. A bullet hit the doorjamb, but it had come from outside the house.

There was another shooter outside somewhere. He prayed that it was Mac.

Cesar ducked inside, taking shelter from this unknown threat, and Trufante scrambled farther out onto the dock.

"Come on, move. I'll cover you. Get the dock lines," a voice muttered from the darkness.

Trufante didn't question the orders. He jumped on the boat and let the lines free as Mac started the engines and slammed the twin diesels into gear. Moments later, they were leaving the harbor, the engines pushing the boat as fast as it could go.

* * *

"Shit. They got away." Cesar quickly inspected himself and, finding no damage, turned to Jose. The large man was writhing in pain on the ground. "I'll get something to wrap that. You'll be okay." He took off his belt, bent down and tightened it around Jose's leg. "Can you get to the truck? I've gotta get rid of the bodies. Police find the same gun was used here as the other house, they'll up the ante."

Jose nodded and started crawling toward the stairs. He used the railing to haul his body erect and limped out the door, a path of blood trailing behind him.

Cesar looked around and saw the crate of diving weights. He stuffed weights into the clothing of the first woman and carried her to the seawall. Once there, he pushed the body off the edge and watched it sink. Then he repeated the procedure with the other woman, dumping her beside her friend, promising the snapper and crabs a few good meals.

He went back inside and turned the lights off. A dark house would attract less attention. The door locked behind him as he went for the truck. He set the lead box on the seat beside him. Ignoring Jose in the backseat, he pulled out of the driveway.

* * *

Mac had slowed the boat as soon as they were out of gunshot range. Mel was on deck now, staring at the two men in shock.

"Can you have a look at his finger?" Mac asked quickly. He spun in the direction of the splash.

"You got anything for the pain?" Trufante whined.

"You're not getting crap until you tell me what the hell is going on here. What just went in the water?"

Trufante went back over the events of the hours since he left the house. Mac and Mel listened intently, glancing at each other as he spoke.

"You've got to be kidding," Mel looked at Trufante. "And you," she looked accusingly at Mac. "You played right along. You seriously need to find another hobby than cleaning up his messes." Another splash interrupted her.

70

"They must be dumping the bodies of those two women. No surprise there — the guy wasn't going to leave those two girls for the cops to find."

"He needs a doctor. Those bastards took his finger off to the knuckle," Mel said.

"No doctors. If we take him to the hospital, the police will be involved. Three people just got shot — two at my place."

"And involving the police would be wrong how?" Mel asked.

"Not yet. Finding that plutonium is more important than answering all their questions. We'll lose hours messing with them."

"Just call Jules. She's the sheriff here - and a friend. She'll know what to do."

"Okay," he said grudgingly. "But I'm still going after the box."

"I'll call Sue. She'll take care of him." Mel's reflexes took her hand to her back pocket, where her phone would have been if she wasn't covered with only a towel.

Mac saw her search and looked at Trufante. He shrugged. "Mine's upstairs."

"You've got that sat phone for emergencies," Trufante held up his digit. "I'd call this one."

Mac went down to the cabin and came back with a black plastic case. He opened it and started up the phone. A quick call to information and he had the number for Fishermen's Hospital. They stared at each other in silence as the waited for Sue to get on the line. Once she answered Mac handed the phone to Trufante.

Chapter 15

Pete watched from the neighbor's house as the truck pulled out of the driveway. He'd heard gunshots and saw the larger man limping out, obviously wounded. His first reaction was to go inside and see if anyone needed help, but then he'd lose the truck. Lights had come on in some of the adjacent houses. Assuming they'd call the police he ran back to his car. Caught up in the adrenaline rush of the night and loyalty to his friends, he decided to follow. He quickly started it up and followed the black truck, with his own lights out, as it pulled out onto US1 heading south. Pete had to wait for several cars and a truck pulling a boat to pass before he could turn. He turned on the headlights as he pulled out and turned left. The black truck was still visible, obeying the speed limit.

He had no trouble following the truck on the two-lane road to Key West. They crossed the Stock Island bridge and turned right onto Business 1 South. Pete followed, staying as close as possible. It was hard to keep enough distance to remain invisible and still not miss any lights. One red light and they were gone. They stayed on North Roosevelt and then turned onto Truman Street. Several blocks later, they took White. Cross traffic was heavy here and Pete had to wait out a dozen cars before he could turn.

The truck was out of sight when he finally made the turn. He cursed to himself, angry at losing them as he drove slowly, craning his neck in both directions as he passed street after street. He was growing discouraged when his phone rang. The number came up with a 305 area code.

"Hello?"

"Pete, is that you? This is Joanie. The bartender told me you were looking for me."

"Hey, how are you?" He put the phone on speaker and set it in his lap as he continued to crane his neck at each intersection.

"Good, just got off work. What's up?"

"I was hoping you were free, but now I'm out for a while." He thought about their night in Key West, and remembered Trufante's disappearance from the bar. "Hey, you know where Tru went in Key West for that stuff?"

She hesitated. "You going to bring me a present? That would be cool."

"Sure. You know where the guy lives?"

"I've been there a couple of times." She gave him directions.

Relief spread over him. "Thanks, I'll call you back in an hour," he said and disconnected.

He backtracked, following her directions, and found the address she'd given him. To his surprise, the truck was in the driveway. He decided it was safer to park several streets over and walk, and found the truck still in the driveway when he arrived.

With no idea what to do now and thinking about the lie he would tell Joanie when he got back, he walked up the neighbor's driveway. Staying out of sight, he worked his way towards the open window on the side of the house.

He crouched under the window, hoping to hear something to explain the craziness. In the last two days he'd found and lost a fortune in drugs. He had no idea where Dan or Jeff where. He'd seen the girls and Trufante go into the house and not come out. Gunshots, drugs ... he was overwhelmed. There were voices now.

"Got it." He could see two shadows through the window. Someone was on the phone. "Yeah, they got into a couple of packages, but I got most of it back." The man paused, then nodded. "The other one, too. Had to do a little work to get that one." The man listened for a minute and answered, "There are still a few loose ends. I'll make the drop, then go back in the morning and clean things up." Another pause, and then, "Okay, name's Ibrahim, got it. Where do I find this dude?"

* * *

Ibrahim rolled up the prayer rug and massaged his leg. There was a massive scar down the front, where the shark had bitten him. He had matching wounds on his side and arm. The shark attack had almost ended his life, but had actually saved him. Without the attack he would have gone after his friend and accomplice, Behzad - may he be in paradise, and likely would have ended up there as well. The two men were discovered in a plot to detonate a nuclear bomb found offshore. His phone buzzed and he looked down and saw an incoming email message.

He went to the computer and logged into his Hotmail account, but the message was nothing. Just a ruse for the NSA robots. He opened the drafts folder and read the note then, smiling, deleted it. The terrorist cell used the draft folder to communicate. That way there was no real communication for the NSA to follow. No meta data to accumulate.

He went to the kitchen to make some tea and, while the water was boiling, popped two pain killers and waited. The pain from his wounds was often unbearable. Allah might not approve of the medication, but he couldn't function and do God's work without them. He longed for the end of his pain and the utopia of paradise.

"Soon, Ibrahim," he told himself gently. He poured the water into a cup, added a tea bag and stared at it. With a look of submission he went to the cabinet over the refrigerator and took out a quarter full bottle of brandy. He drank from the bottle. He needed the alcohol to mitigate the pain while the pain relievers took effect. He followed this pattern more than he prayed.

He waited, anxious for the phone to ring and the pain to disappear, although he knew it wouldn't. As if Allah had answered his prayer it rang. The phone was a burner, a prepaid untraceable cell phone. He expected the man on the other end used similar precautions but kept the conversation inert anyway. Meeting arranged, he sat and drank his tea, dreaming of an end to his pain and the virgins in paradise. For the thousandth time, he reviewed the new plan, and thought about what he'd do when he gained possession of the plutonium. Then he picked up another cell — one of the three he currently used — and dialed a number in Dearborn, Michigan.

Chapter 16

Jeff drove like a demon, making the eight-hour drive to Tampa in five, a full two hours quicker than his best time. He almost wished he'd been pulled over, so he could tell someone what had happened. He'd thought of stopping at every exit and telling the authorities what had happened, but was terrified of losing his wife. His mind was racing and his body ached from sitting so long, unable to release the tension in his muscles. He replayed the scene from the house over and over ... still not understanding it. It happened so fast, he was having trouble understanding what had happened and why. But before he knew it, he was home. He pulled into his driveway and sat there, decompressing from the drive. Director of the Army Retirement Services at MacDill Air Force Base, he was a civilian employee in charge of payroll and pensions. His position allowed access to money and he'd come up with a plan. There was a good chance he could even get away with it. He plotted the sequence of events necessary to funnel off the money.

Not due back from vacation for another three days, he couldn't waltz in now, sit down, and start punching buttons. He'd have to at least wait until the morning, fabricate some kind of emergency and show up as if to save the day.

Sleep eluded him as he knew it would. He tossed and turned for the five hours he actually tried. Around dawn, with a couple hours more to kill, he gave up and went for a jog. Last night he had thought his plan could work, now after the long night he had played Devil's advocate, he tried to repair the holes punched in it as he ran the quiet streets of his suburban neighborhood. Thirty minutes later he was back in the house. He showered, dressed, and headed for the base.

It was easier than he thought to reach the sanctuary of his office. His secretary had the same vacation time, and she would have been the only obstacle. Desperate, he chanced the kitchen, grabbed a cup of coffee, and then shut himself in his office. His palms were sweating as he turned on his computer, ignoring the multitude of emails that had accumulated, and got to work.

First he opened the screen to enter a new account. Fictitious information started to fill the page as he typed: entering a false name, rank, and service history. His personal bank account and social security number were entered in the appropriate fields. He glanced constantly at the door, expecting an MP to enter, gun drawn, at any time. An hourglass spun on the screen as the online form was processed. The screen refreshed, showing the account number of a Colonel Joseph Roberts, retired. He double-checked the information and started fabricating his pension payments. With more time, he could funnel off a thousand a week without setting off alarms. But, with the hours left until they killed his wife, he had to do it in one shot — a hundred-thousand-dollar shot. And he had no idea what kind of oversight they had on this sort of thing, or whether it would raise any red flags. Still, what choice did he have?

Five minutes later, he checked the screen. The account was funded. He logged off his work computer and went for his smart phone, where he logged into his bank account and checked the balance. The money was listed as pending. Assuming it wouldn't post until the next day, he headed back to his car. A visit with the bank manager might help make the funds available more quickly. If not he'd just have to be late. It was all he could do.

* * *

He was almost out the door when a hand clasped his shoulder.

"Hey, buddy, got a minute?" The uniformed officer's grip turned him 180 degrees, and they walked together toward the security office. "Why don't you have seat? The brass wants you for something."

Jeff's hopes plummeted. This was his only shot at getting his wife back. He'd watched the Columbian shoot Dan, and had no doubt he would do so again, this time to his wife. But if his subterfuge was discovered already, there was no way he could save her life.

He sat in the chair staring vacantly at the wall for what seemed like an eternity, the options running through his head. His only chance was to find a receptive ear and tell his story. As a civilian employee he was not regulated by the UCMJ. The Uniform Code of Military Justice applied to military personnel only. What he had done was a felony in the real world and he feared prosecution there. He worried that drugs were involved, but compared to hijacking one hundred thousand dollars from the government's pension fund, that was a non-starter. Just losing his job was now a best case scenario.

He finally came to a solution he could live with: He'd have to tell the truth and insist they keep the girls safe. Then he'd pay whatever penalty the Army cared to enforce.

"Jeff, come on in," the officer called him into his office. "You got a story you want to tell me? The Army may not be very good about keeping track of some things, but a transfer of that size? Come on, man, someone has to see it."

"It was my only hope." Jeff put his head in his hands, tears forming.

"Take your time. The colonel should be here in a minute."

Jeff panicked, "You've got to understand. My wife's life is at stake. If I don't get this money to Marathon by tonight, she's dead."

"Hold on, son." The officer stopped him and pressed a

button on his phone. "Get the colonel here, now. I don't care if you need to shake it for him. Now." He hung up and glanced at Jeff. "You're one of us, Jeff. Hell, you've been handling my retirement for years. You may not know it, but we all know who you are. And we take care of ours."

Jeff leaned forward in the chair, cradling his head in his hands. His world was crumbling around him.

The colonel walked in the door. "Jeff, you in some kind of trouble?"

Jeff starred at the floor as he poured out the whole story. A wave of relief passed though him now that it was in the open. He looked up at the colonel, awaiting his fate.

"Go back to your office and undo what you've done. Clean it all up. You're in luck, I know the sheriff down there in Marathon, served with her for a few years. Think we can probably get her on board, get this figured out. Let me make a call. I'll come up to your office as soon as I talk to her. Don't worry."

Jeff eased back in the chair and stared at the ceiling for a minute before he trusted his shaking legs to get him out the door.

* * *

Pete sat motionless in the bushes. His feet and knees had gone numb maintaining his position. It was just past daylight and the house was quiet now. His courage had faded as the sun rose. He was resigned to taking what he had to the police and hoping they'd just let him go when the door opened. He watched as the guy Trufante had called Cesar made for the truck, started up, and pulled out of the driveway. As soon as the headlights swung the other way, he sprinted for his car. Wherever the guy was heading, he hoped he could catch up to him. He knew it wasn't rational, but he was proud of himself for getting this far.

The truck's brake lights were visible at the intersection just as Pete pulled out. He accelerated, hoping to make up some ground, and reached the intersection seconds after the truck turned right onto Truman. He waited out the traffic, now confident he'd be able to follow. The truck turned right on First Street and left on Flagler. Jeff stayed as far back as he could, his lone headlight illuminating the way. Ahead of him, the truck turned right on Government and then into Little Hamaca Park. He parked and waited, watching as a pink scooter approached the truck.

* * *

"That your scooter? Nice ride," Cesar said through the open window. A gun rested below his thigh just in case the exchange went awry.

"A friend's. You have my package?"

"Yeah." Cesar handed the box through the window.

"You're not worried about being seen here?" the other guy asked.

Cesar snorted. "Fuck. This is the homeless capital of the universe. The police don't come near this place after dark."

"Suit yourself." Ibrahim took the offered box and examined it. Satisfied, he put it in the basket of the scooter and pulled out.

Cesar exhaled as the window closed. He adjusted the air-conditioning to high, realizing that he was sweating. He put the truck in reverse and pulled out, thankful the exchange was done.

* * *

Pete watched the men from the cover of an overgrown hibiscus bush. He'd left the car out of sight as soon as he saw the black truck pull over and followed on foot. Several homeless people snorted at him as he passed their cardboard abodes, but he ignored them. He saw the drug dealer hand the lead box to the guy on the scooter. Hoping the trail was coming to an end, he decided to follow the scooter.

Chapter 17

Seven Hundred Eleventh Street was a prestigious address, the top floor of the building even more so. Patel stared past the man at the desk and out the office window taking in the view from the thirteenth and top floor, a partial view of the White House in the distance. The flamboyant wealth displayed by these infidels disgusted him. Although his carefully crafted exterior appearance matched the surroundings, he was different inside. Raised Akim Hullah in Saudi Arabia, he had been sent to the United States to attend college years ago. Remaining after law school, he had climbed the ladder at Davies and Associates, manipulating cases as he could, but mostly, biding his time for something bigger.

He looked at Bradley Davies, founder and managing partner of Davies and Associates.

Patel knew the history. Davies had parted ways with the ACLU in the 1980s. He'd shared many of their views but was tired of having his cases shot down. Unable to climb the ladder and reach a coveted seat on the board of directors, where he could pick his own cases, he left. A membership organization, the ACLU was more interested in making political hay than money. Davies and Associates was interested in both, often leaning toward cases that were important but had large damages attached to them. It was the best of both worlds.

"The delivery was lost," Patel said.

"No big deal. Send out another one."

"You know how long it took to get that? Those men you say you trust in Florida, if they are captured, will leave behind records."

"Those guys won't give up anything. In their culture it's a badge of honor to keep quiet."

"Even if they keep quiet. One record. An email. A phone call...."

"Relax. They called here. I am their attorney and represented their leader, Diego years ago. He's on our client roster. That will ensure attorney-client privilege. He won't talk."

They were interrupted by Patel's phone. He listened intently, using his free hand to signal to Davies that he needed something to write with. Pad in hand, he wrote out an address.

"We have a lead. The man got away, but this is the address."

Davies looked at the pad. It took a minute for it to register. He'd seen this address on countless overnight envelopes over the last few months. This was where Mel was staying. When he dialed, her phone went straight to voicemail.

"Interesting. Somehow one of my attorneys is mixed up in this."

Patel looked at him accusingly. "Melanie?"

Davies nodded.

"Simple, then. Get her to get it back."

"Not so simple. Currently she's more loyal to that boyfriend of hers than to me."

"There are other ways," Patel said. "Tell me about this man. Can we use him as leverage to get her to cooperate?"

"Name's Travis, Mac Travis. Been down there for years living off the land in typical Keys fashion. Strong minded guy, just like her father. This guy is invisible. I've had a PI run down the basic stuff on him, and the numbers don't add up. He's pulling in a marginal income fishing and doing commercial dive work, but it doesn't add up. He pays his taxes, but has no bank accounts. He paid cash for his house and boat. That's probably five hundred thousand for the house and another two for the boat." Davies summarized. He had acquired the information in an effort to get Travis to testify, now it served another purpose. "What do you have in mind?"

"FISA warrants are rubber stamps. Get one on him. It'll turn up something."

"What are you looking for?"

"Emails and phone records."

"I'll see what I can do."

STEVEN BECKER

Chapter 18

Mac pulled back on the throttles and looked over his shoulder as the boat backed up to an empty dock by Fifty-First Street. Sue ran over to the seawall as Mac and Mel helped Trufante over the transom and onto the dock.

"Patch him up and keep him at your place." Mac was on the dock holding the boat with one line. "No hospital, no police. I guess you know the drill."

"Do you look for trouble or does it just find you?" she asked both men. "I don't know if he keeps me around because he likes me or because I can fix him."

Trufante grabbed her ass, answering her question.

"Here." She handed Mac a phone. "You owe me fifty for it. I put my cell number in. Let me know when it's safe."

"Thanks. Take care of him."

Mac jumped back on the boat, took the helm, and handed the phone to Mel. They watched Sue take Trufante to her car and waited for her to pull out before they moved. Then Mac put the boat in gear and headed out toward Boot Key Harbor. They rode in silence, waiting for open water before they started talking. Mac bit his lip. Mel wasn't going to like what he had to say.

As usual, Mel beat him to the punch. "I assume you're not going back to your place. Go ahead, spit it out. What are you two in now?"

He put up a cautionary hand. "Sound does strange things in these canals, and you never know who's staying aboard one of these boats." He cocked his head to the seawall, which was lined with boats. "Seas are down, I'm gonna head out to the lighthouse

84

and anchor up on a mooring buoy over night. We can talk when we get out there."

He idled past the condos and hotels backing on the seawall. Boats were anchored along it, some with lights on, muted conversation barely audible. He turned left into the mangrove-lined canal leading to Sisters Creek, and hit the throttle. Five minutes later, the boat was in open water, running smoothly toward the lighthouse. Once there, he tied off to one of the mooring balls — frequented by tourist and dive charters during the day but mostly vacant at night. The closest boat was a quarter mile away, and he thought they'd be safe.

Swallowing heavily, he went down to talk to Mel.

* * *

"What the hell, Mac, what are you mixed up in now?"

"It's Trufante. He came to me with this box, part of one of his drug deals. Some tourists were out fishing and hooked a square grouper. They took it thinking they were gonna get rich and now it's snowballed. There were fifty bricks: forty-nine coke and one different. It was a lead box soldered shut." He had her attention now. "I started small, but ended up cutting it open. It was loaded with plutonium, looked like weapons grade stuff. I repackaged it with some industrial material from an old compaction tester. It's radioactive, but harmless compared to the other stuff. I put the box back in the safe. I think I must have left it open when you came down last night. Anyway, I don't know what the deal was with those guys and the women, but it doesn't take much to guess that it has to do with that box. They must have tortured Tru, got him to admit that the box was at my house. That's all I know."

"So the Hispanic guy is gone? With a box of...."

"It's harmless now. Hopefully that'll buy us some time."

"Where's the real stuff?"

Mac went forward and came back with the lead coated ball. He went to hand it to her, but she recoiled.

"Now what?"

"Tomorrow I'm taking this to a spot I know and stashing it 'till we can figure out what's going on here."

"Have you called Jules?" She gave him her lawyer look. "You promised."

"Yeah, I know, I'll call now." He picked up the burner phone Sue had left. "Wish I had my phone now."

"That's a good one." She laughed and headed towards the cabin.

He stayed on deck, calling information and then the sheriff's office. The dispatcher said that Jules was out. He left a message and set the phone down.

Sleep was not even close and alcohol was not the answer tonight. Too much to figure out. He sat on the deck and watched the sky, waiting for the sun to rise.

* * *

"Sheriff Whitman," Jules answered, golf club resting on her hip.

"Jules, Dave Rayburn. Been forever."

"Yeah, it has. What can I do for you?" Julie Whitman had been sheriff of this corner of paradise long enough to know that most calls from old friends were for favors.

"Got a guy that works for me in some big-time trouble down there."

Whitman's attitude changed at that. Trouble was her specialty. "Tell me what you have."

Rayburn told her everything he knew. She was silent as he told of the fake transfer and abduction. When he was done, the line was silent. "Jules?"

"I'm here, just thinking. Can you get him down here fast? I need this firsthand."

"I can put him on the puddle jumper to Key West. Be there about one o'clock."

"That's fine. Tell him I'll pick him up there. That'll give me some time to figure this out. One more thing. I need the address of the house they were staying at."

"I'll get him on the plane and text it to you. Listen, he's a good guy. Think he's just mixed up in a dirty deal. Any help I can give you, just call. I'll do whatever I can."

"You got it. I'll keep you posted."

She'd grown up here and knew the Keys were a major point of entry for drug smugglers. The chain of islands was impossible to patrol by boat, especially the Gulf side with all the unmarked channels and small keys. Any smart smuggler knew to use a fishing boat and blend in with the local traffic. Because there was so much volume going through here, the dealers here were worse than your dime-store drug dealer. If this guy had gotten mixed up with one of them, this was going to be bad.

She dialed her office as she walked, assembling people and assets to get a handle on this thing. A CSI, the coroner, then a couple of deputies and maybe a helicopter to Key West to pick up the witness. The numbers were crunching in her head. Her ever-shrinking budget was about to go under water. She hated that part of her job and tended to ignore it, doing the right thing first and paying for it later as the city council expressed their dissatisfaction.

Chapter 19

The alarm on the GPS beeped, and Mac signaled Mel to throw the buoy out. The ball splashed the water, the reel spinning, spitting out line until the five pound weight rested on the bottom. He started circling the buoy slowly, carefully watching the depth finder for the right piece of bottom. This section of reef was live bottom — small ledges with sand trenches between them. Common throughout the area, most areas looked the same. Red and black humps marked the hard coral and rocks, while yellow marked the sand on the display. Landmarks were few, making it an art to find a particular rock. But Mac had been here enough to identify the three coral heads clumped together, rising five feet off the three-foot ledge. As soon as the image came onto the screen, he had Mel throw another buoy. The GPS waypoint signaled by the alarm only got within thirty to sixty feet, depending on the alignment and signal of the satellites. The second buoy was necessary to mark the exact spot. He steered back toward the first buoy and she pulled it from the water, using the reel to wind the hundred and ten feet of line on until the weight was retrieved.

He nudged the throttle and adjusted course slightly bringing the boat to the second buoy. Mac put the engines in neutral and sat for a minute to see which way the current was running in order to see which way the boat would drift. Ideally the anchor would set right on the coral heads allowing him to follow the line straight to his destination, rather than waste precious bottom time searching. Satisfied he hit the switch for the windlass, which automatically dropped the anchor. Line spun out as he backed down. With the proper scope set out, he stopped and went forward to check if the hook had set. Satisfied, he started to assemble his dive gear.

"I don't like you going down by yourself."

"Get certified, then. I'd love the company."

"What's the deal with the tank?" she asked.

"It's Nitrox. Enriched air. It's got a higher oxygen content and less nitrogen. Lets you go deeper longer."

"That sounds really reassuring."

"No worries, girl. I've been using this stuff for a long time. It's just safer at this depth. I can get forty minutes of bottom time, compared to fourteen with regular air."

Minutes later, Mac sat on the gunwale, gave Mel the thumbs up sign, and rolled backwards into the water, lead ball in his hand. The water rippled out in rings as he entered, broken only by the boat as he finned toward the anchor line and followed it down. The bottom quickly became visible — with no current and the sun's help, the visibility was about eighty feet. He took his time descending, clearing his ears as he went. After checking the anchor, he took a bearing on his compass and set out toward the east.

The ledge protruded from the sand about three feet, coral heads scattered in islands in front of it, small fish schooled everywhere. He ignored the scenery, searching for the familiar landmarks, and swam toward a rise in the structure, where three coral heads sat directly on top of the ledge, rising eight feet above the bottom. From there, he got down on the sand and unstrapped the tank from his back. The weighted BC held the tank on the bottom, and he unclipped the dive light from the BC and illuminated the coral.

He reached under the ledge and removed the two rocks covering the entrance to the small cavern. A huge black grouper had taken his spear into the hole several years earlier and he'd gone in and wrestled the fish, discovering the cavern in the process. He'd kept it in mind ever since, in case he ever needed a hiding place. Now the light illuminated the interior. It was about three feet high, and not quite big enough for a man to fit in, but a great secret spot. The light revealed several round canisters and a dry bag held down with weights. Not a pirate's treasure chest, but a collection of Mac's secrets. He placed the lead ball in and moved back out, closing the entrance behind him.

* * *

Mac broke the surface of the water thirty minutes later relieving her tension. She knew he had enough experience to dive himself, but anything could happen down there.

He hauled himself onto the dive platform, taking off his BC and tank. "Done. That's as safe as it's gonna get."

She nodded. "Talked to Sue. Tru's ok. Not much she can do but keep the wound clean and make sure there's no infection. She's got him pumped up on pain killers and antibiotics. I swear I thought he was singing in the background."

Mac climbed over the transom. "She could be the perfect girl for that boy. Puts up with his crap and can fix him when he's broke."

"Is that what it takes to be the perfect woman?"

"You got it, babe." He punched her shoulder as he went by.

"What now?"

"Gotta deal with the house. Then we'll try and pick up the pieces."

She watched him stow his gear thinking how her quick trip to appear in court had gone awry.

* * *

Pete had to stay closer to the scooter than he would have liked. There must have been a thousand pink scooters in Key West, many ridden by packs of tourists. It would be easy to lose one on Duval Street. The guy had turned onto the tourist mecca now and was cruising slowly, dodging drunks as he went. Pete watched, two car lengths back, as the scooter turned onto a street and pulled into a driveway where the man got off. Address noted, he cruised by and kept going, driving aimlessly until he worked his way back toward the south end of the island. The road finally dead ended into a beach, and he sat there staring at the water.

There was something weirder than a drug deal going on here. He had no idea what had happened at the house earlier. Trufante and the women were there when the gunshots were fired. With nothing to lose, he dialed Trufante's number, cursing when it went straight to voicemail. He tried a text, hoping that might get him an answer. He stared at Joanie's number in the recent calls log, paralyzed by what he'd seen in the last few hours. He'd watched his deal go south, been shot at, and had followed a lunatic to Key West. The guy had then met some Islamic-looking guy with something that had nothing to do with drugs. This was way over his pay grade now. "Why not?" he thought, as he stared at the recent call log. He hit her number.

Joanie wasn't the answer to the puzzle, but she answered her phone, excited he'd called. He told her he'd be back in Marathon in an hour. Yes, she'd love to see him. At that, a smile crossed his face for the first time all day.

The adrenaline had run it's course and he felt lost. He knew enough to go to the police, but he'd been up all night and didn't want to face the interrogation he would surely receive. Whatever damage had been done to Trufante and the girls was already done. There was nothing he could do to help them now. He resolved to go to the police in the morning.

Chapter 20

Heather looked around the room, camera around her neck and notebook in hand. There was a metallic scent in the air. She looked for it's source and immediately keyed in on the blood soaked couch. The two officers already there had just turned the crime scene over to the CSI people. Or person, as it was in understaffed Monroe County. The coroner was pushing the gurney with the man's body out the door.

"Can you run through it for me?" she asked the first man she saw.

The younger officer — the one without the wedding band — was quick to respond. "Sure." He gave her a big smile. "The dude was shot — looks like point blank range — right here." He pointed to the couch. "There's evidence of at least four other people in the house — two couples and a single guy, from the looks of it. Not much of a struggle."

Heather scanned the room, trying to figure out where to start. "Okay, I got it from here."

The officer's grin faded as it became apparent she wasn't interested, and his partner smacked him on the back of the head. "I know you're new here, but that's the sheriff's girl. Got no shot with that one, buddy. On the other team."

Heather shook her head and settled into the scene, trying to recreate what had happened. She moved through the house, camera clicking, stopping now and then to look at some barely visible fiber or clue, bagging them as she went. The couch had a blood spot the size of a melon where the victim's head had been. She took several pictures of the spot, with and without a measuring tape in place.

There was a hole toward the center of the patch of blood. She set down the camera, took a multi-tool off her belt and, knife extended, started probing the couch, grinning when the knife hit resistance in the foam. She got in closer, drew the slug out, bagged and tagged it, placing it by the casing she'd found earlier.

* * *

Jeff staggered out of the terminal building, shielding his eyes from the sunlight. He made his way to the sheriff's car parked in the shade of an overhang, thinking that you had to have a cherry on top to get a spot like that. The passenger-side window of the car rolled down, releasing a blast of cool air as he approached.

"You Jeff Bundt?" asked the woman sitting in the car, sun glasses shielding her eyes, auburn hair blowing from the air conditioning.

"Yeah."

"I'm the sheriff from Marathon. Just call me Jules; we're casual around here. Get in."

He was uncertain until the woman kicked open the passenger door. Once inside, she motioned for him to buckle up and pulled away from the curb. He sat motionless, staring straight forward as if awaiting an interrogation he expected to start any second.

"Easy, son. The colonel told me you were alright, just in some trouble. I want to help you get your wife and the other woman back. We're gonna head back up to Marathon, but I need to know what we're looking at here. Take your time and start from the beginning. I want every detail you can think of."

She waited until they were off the island, heading north on US1 before she started asking questions. Jeff recounted the story for the second time that day. He tried to stay focused through her constant interruptions to clarify details. Finally satisfied she stared at the road ahead, leaving him to wonder what was going through her mind. Exhausted, he sank back in the seat, set his head against the headrest and closed his eyes.

Not sure if she were determined to not let him rest, or if she were just processing everything he'd told her she cleared her throat.

"What now, Sheriff?"

"Call me Jules, everyone else does. Once we get back to Marathon, I'll sit you down with some mug shots and see if you can identify either of the guys you saw. Don't worry, it's not like the big city police shows. We've got a much smaller collection here. Then we'll see if the detectives or CSI came up with anything at the murder scene. Other than that, we wait 'til he contacts you, then play it by ear."

"That's it? Mug shots and sit and wait?"

"If we can identify him, we can get the jump on him. We'll be in a better position that way. Maybe send a SWAT team in. If we *can't* ID him, we're playing more on his turf. But be assured, he *will* open himself up at some point. He wants the money, not the hostages. Which means he'll get in touch with you."

"If it's a hostage situation, shouldn't the FBI be called in?"

"Technically, but the agent down here is a big time douche. I guarantee this will have a bad outcome if he's involved."

"I'll leave that up to you."

* * *

Heather walked into the room without knocking, urgency in her step. "Got something."

"Already? Good work." Jules smiled at her. Jeff stood off to the side, studying her wall of plaques and awards

"We know this guy. Cesar Vasquez. Drugs, all kinds of stuff. I got a partial print off the casing and ran it. Came back with his name. I'm still working on the slug."

"Good work, Heather, keep me posted."

Jules pushed her sunglasses back on her head and called in two deputies. She waited at her desk for them to arrive. Murder in Marathon was not typical. One side of her relished the challenge of solving the case; the other was pissed that it had happened on her turf. She promised herself, whoever had committed it would pay.

The men entered. "This guy's bad news. Not entirely stable. Can one of you contact his parole officer - he's got to have one. Been in and out a bunch of times. See if you can get an address for him." She turned to Jeff. "You want to hang out here, you're welcome. If you want to call someone, you're free to go."

"I'll hang out, if you don't mind. If there's anything I can do, please let me know."

"Why don't you go through the mug shots and see if you can ID the other guy? Anything will help. I got a feeling our friend Cesar is in Key West. If he hung around anywhere from Islamorada to Big Pine Key, I'd know him by now. I'm going down there."

* * *

Heather set him up at a computer monitor. "Not your grandma's mug shot book." She showed him how to scroll through the pictures, then left him alone.

Jeff sat down and went to work. He was distracted by the activity going on around him. For the first time in two days he felt a sense of order. Unfortunately this allowed his mind to wander. He hadn't faced the reality yet that the girls might be dead. It felt like a start to have a name for the guy now. If this guy, Cesar, had killed Dan like that there was no telling what his wife was going through.

He was still scanning mug shots a half hour later. Each picture had started to look like the one before. He scrolled to the next screen and suddenly sat up, fully alert. It was the teeth that set this one apart. He was the guy they'd dragged into the house with them. There was no mistaking him. He yelled for Heather.

She came up behind him. "Got something?"

"That guy. He was there. Not one of the bad guys, I don't think. He was hurt too."

"Alan Trufante. I'll tell the sheriff. Figures he's mixed up in this." She pulled out her cell phone and punched in a number, then put it to her ear. "You're not going to believe this. He ID'd Trufante." She listened to her instructions, then nodded and hung up. "I'm going to see if I can get a lead on him, find out where he is. Want to tag along?"

"Sure. You know this guy?"

"Everyone that's been around here for a while knows him. Not a bad guy, but he's got a knack for finding trouble. Looks like he stepped in it again."

Jeff sat back with a sense of accomplishment.

She grabbed the keys for her cruiser from a peg by the door. They were out of the station now. It was cooler, the sun moving behind the buildings, casting long shadows. Heather got in an unmarked car, and Jeff went around and got in the passenger seat.

"Where're we going?" he asked.

"Gonna start at this bar he frequents. Bartender there is a friend of mine. If he's not there, she'll know where to find him."

Chapter 21

Patel went straight from the plane to the airport restroom. He went to a stall, opened his carry-on and removed a mirror and fake beard. A quick change of clothes and he looked like a different man. Ibrahim was waiting for him at the baggage claim at Miami International as he had directed. They shook hands and smiled, knowing that their mission, after months of waiting, was about to happen. He'd already failed once and was committed to success this time.

"Let's get your bags and get out of here. There are cameras everywhere," Ibrahim said to the bearded man

"Allah willing, they do not have us on record." He was sure he was not, taking precautions every time he travelled.

The suitcases started around the carousel. The men waited patiently as the tourists reached over each other and scrambled for their bags. Before long, the stainless steel case they were waiting for came through the plastic strips and started moving around the belt.

"Couldn't you use something a little less conspicuous?" Ibrahim murmured.

"It is exactly that. Making it conspicuous makes it work. A bag like that, you know they are going to x-ray. There is a lead casing half the size of the suitcase inside. Placed around the compartment is everything you would expect in a bag. They see that and let it go. Inside the lead chamber, they cannot see."

"Very good." Ibrahim looked impressed. The glass doors to the parking area opened with a swoosh. They were assaulted by the steam rising off the baked concrete. It had just rained and now the sun was creating a steam bath. Bag in hand, they headed out the doors to the car Ibrahim had rented for the trip.

Ibrahim pulled into the light traffic and then merged onto the 836 heading west. They sat in silence until he pulled off at the last exit before the Florida Turnpike. He stopped in a parking lot and reached for a roll of electric tape in the center console.

"Why are we stopping. It is urgent that we evaluate the material as soon as possible."

"We need to change the numbers on the license plates." The man seemed satisfied they were taking precautions and said nothing further. Ibrahim got out and removed the tape already in place. The eight returned to a three. He added two strips of tape to the one, turning it into a four. The procedure was repeated on the front plate. Before he got back in he checked the SunPass receptor on the roof, making sure the tape was still in place. It was no longer possible to pay cash at the two tolls between Miami and Florida City. When the SunPass did not register a camera would photograph the license plates. Changing the plates would buy him some time, he thought, if the infidels were looking for him.

The ride south was uneventful. Ibrahim kept to the speed limit after restoring the license plates to their original numbers in Key Largo. Three hours later they pulled into his driveway.

In the living room, the man opened the case and removed the lead box, which contained the tools of his trade. Screwdrivers, wire cutters, voltage meter, and a geiger counter were visible, along with a pile of less-recognizable items. He took out the jeweler's loupe and packed the rest away.

Now he set his palms down on the table and leaned toward the box. "Let's see what we've got here." He held the box with one hand and inspected each side with a magnifying glass. Suddenly he stopped. "Here. This should not be here."

Ibrahim looked over his shoulder. "What?"

"That spot. The solder is new, and different." He scraped the solder spot with his finger. "Definitely not original work." He rotated the box carefully, inspecting it. "But nothing else is out of place. Do you have the gear I asked for?"

"Upstairs." The man followed Ibrahim to the bedroom. Ibrahim removed a plastic-wrapped exposure suit from the back of his closet. "Easier than I thought to get one of these. All the preppers think they need them, so they're all over the internet. It's not for long-term exposure, but it should do the job."

"Good, we will need that later. You have the room ready?"

"I used the closet." He pointed at the closed door. "I know you prefer a basement, but they don't have them here."

They entered the room, and the bearded man looked around. The walls and ceiling were lined with lead sheets, twenty-four inches wide, overlapped at each seam. The floor was covered in plywood; dull metal was visible at the seams. Even the back of the door was covered."Very well done, my friend. Please bring my equipment up, and I will get to work."

Ibrahim went downstairs, gathered tools from the table and paused. He had not had a dose of his pain medication in hours. Quickly he moved to the kitchen and repeated his ritual: two pills followed by a shot from the brandy bottle.

The man took the tools and placed them on the table. Next he carefully took the box and set it in the vise clamped to the table. He started the Dremel tool, its blade whizzing, and then whining as he carefully inserted it into the solder joint. The solder cut easily, and he moved around the box, reseting the clamp as necessary. Several minutes later, he removed the lid and inspected the contents. "This has been tampered with. How is that possible?"

"I do not know, my friend. What do you mean, tampered?"

"Look." He held the geiger counter over the box. "It is barely showing anything. The correct material would have the needle all the way in the red."

"That is not possible. It was delivered last night by the contact we agreed on."

"Get him here. Now."

* * *

Cesar was cleaning his gun when the phone rang. He set the barrel down, picked up the phone and listened. Without saying a word in return he cursed under his breath and finished his work. Always problems. It was bad enough with just the drugs, but now these rag heads were involved. He again questioned his cousin's judgment. The drug money was big, so why branch out? The gun reassembled, he placed it in his waistband. A shoulder holster was preferable, but jackets in Key West were saved for the three days a year when the temperature got below seventy.

Parking would be a nightmare around the other house, so he decided to walk the dozen blocks. The time and exercise would do him good. Besides, Ibrahim was too upset when he called, and it would be better to let him cool down. Cesar didn't react to emotion well. A more business-like approach was more to his liking. He crossed the street, ignoring the constant stream of bicycles and people. He didn't blend in with the freak show, so why bother.

Ibrahim opened the door just as he was about to knock. "Come in. Hurry. What took you so long?"

"Easy, *hombre*. I'm here." It seemed that the time lapse had *not* calmed Ibrahim down, and Cesar wondered briefly what had him so worked up. He was a terrorist, wasn't he supposed to have nerves of steel or something? "What's the problem?"

"The box has been tampered with. The material is not the same."

"What do you want from me? I delivered the box to you ... that was my job."

"Your job? Do you realize what you have done. How could you be so careless?"

Cesar reached behind his back but thought better of it.

Shooting the man would not help his standing with Diego. "Listen, sand monkey. I was told to bring the box to you and that is what I have done." His temper had reached it's boiling point.

"This is in both of our interests to straighten this out. We both have men we have to report to. Working together might help us both."

Cesar stopped seething and evaluated what the man had said. "Alright. Things got a little out of hand in the recovery, and the package passed through some unexpected hands before I was able to get it to you. Maybe something happened."

"Allah will be merciful as long as we recover the correct material. Retribution will come to those that have stood in our way."

"*Si*, retribution … I like that. Now you're talking my language. I got a good idea where they are." He turned as if to leave.

"That's all? You have an idea. What are you going to do about it?"

"Don't you worry your sandy head about that. I'll be in touch."

"We do this together. You have proven to be inept."

Chapter 22

Mac pulled the boat up to the lone pile and looped a line around it while Mel went to the stern and tossed a small anchor as far as she could, pulling the line until it buried itself in the sand. The tide would be changing in an hour and without the two points of connection, the boat would swing around with the changing current and ground itself. She scanned the small Key her father had called home. Her brow furrowed, her only outward expression of the sorrow she felt. The island looked deserted, at least, and they jumped over the gunwale, landing in a foot of water.

"This place needs a driveway," Mel said.

Mac laughed. "Well, it's yours now, remodel at will."

At that, she started tearing up. It was hard to see this place without thinking of her dad. This had been his home for close to twenty-five years, built on a hump of coral and sand, five miles from the rest of the world. She was in a bad place: tense from being shot at and sullen about seeing her dad's place. Both of them had been anxious to get away from Mac's house where the murders had apparently taken place. They'd agreed on the way back from the reef that this was the safest place. Taking only enough time at Mac's to grab their phones, clothes, and supplies, they'd locked up and headed under the Seven Mile Bridge toward the Gulf towards Wood's island, where they hoped they'd be safe, at least for the time being.

Mel watched as Mac removed the scrub covering the path and started for the house. One hundred feet in, a clearing opened up, mangroves creeping in at the edges, and they saw the house. It was boarded up, plywood covering the windows and doors. Mac went for the shed and plugged a new battery into the cordless drill. He checked the charge, hoping the solar system — the only source of power here — was still operating. Satisfied, he headed up the stairs to the porch, Mel behind him.

"Thanks for boarding it up," she murmured.

"We got that hurricane warning last fall. Figured I better. Wood had all the plywood cut, drilled, and stacked. Was pretty easy." He started removing the screws from the 3/4" thick plywood sheet covering the front door. The wood removed, they entered the house.

Mel nearly choked on the smell of the place. "It's a sauna in here."

"Give me a minute, I'll get some of the windows opened up, get some air flow."

It cooled quickly. The breeze hit the sweat on her body, instantly cooling her. The house breathed well. Wood had used a passive solar design to capture the consistent southerly breeze. The large eaves shielded the windows from the unrelenting sun.

Mac had gone, she assumed, to stow the plywood sheets. She pulled out her phone and connected with the world again.

* * *

"You've got to be kidding me," she snapped. She'd been listening for a few minutes. Mac had come in and she'd given him the *go away* look.

"No," Bradley Davies said. "We have a source in the NSA. Looks like your boyfriend is involved in some strange stuff. I'm just putting the pieces together. Now I know why he won't testify."

Mel snarled, seeing through the lie immediately. "That bastard Patel did this. What's he after? I know he wants to use this case to get publicity for himself. This isn't over. Just because the president comes out and says they won't use drones on American soil doesn't mean squat. If they exist, someone will use them. This needs to go in front of a court to get the word out. I want legislation to come out of this. Not some vague promise from a mealy-mouthed politician."

"Mel, calm down," Davies said. "You're just going to have to put your ego on the bench and play with the team here."

"It's not my ego! It's Patel. He's been trying to push his own agenda since you opened the door and let him in."

"You want out anyway. Why not just testify, and we can part ways? Sometimes you've got to know when it's over."

"After everything we've been through? Now you too! You've been like a father to me."

"And you're turning into your father, and that doesn't fit with us anymore."

"Do *not* call me my father. I'm not dropping this." She hung up and started pacing.

* * *

"The NSA has everything. Phone records, recorded calls, emails — all of it. What are you hiding from me?"

"I'm not hiding anything," Mac tried to soothe her.

"Whether I believe you or not, they have enough to discredit me and you as witnesses. They'll tie us together and put a bow on it. I'm so deep in this drone thing that they'll think I made it all up, and that's the end of the case and my career. Davies has been warning me not to get personally involved. Maybe he was right."

"I was there, Mel, I saw what happened. They can't say it didn't."

"Whatever. It doesn't matter. If they can discredit you as a witness, they will. I want to know what's in those emails." Her face softened slightly, "I can help you."

"There's nothing there. I get all kinds of emails and calls from all kinds of people. They want me to dive for salvage for them. I do have a reputation here. That's got to be all it is."

"Why all the secrecy, then?"

"That's the way they work. They all think they're going to

find the next Atocha or hit oil. Every one of them has an angle and they are not always on the up and up." He looked hurt. "I guess you were right to be paranoid about someone reading emails."

"Clear it up and testify then. I can take over as lead council and throw that slime ball Patel out on his butt."

He walked toward her, hoping to calm her down, but she resisted his touch. "We've been through this. I'm not going to do it. Screw them and whatever they think they have on me."

"Sometime in your life you're going to have to take a stand about something. You can't fish a couple of days a week and think that what's going on in the world is not going to effect you. That's naive."

"You sure you want to go there?"

"Yes." She glared at him, her dander up. "Don't you get it? Drones, NSA snooping. It's death by a thousand pinpricks. Somewhere you have to draw the line and send them a message."

She was dug in now and he knew it but couldn't stop. His frustration, built up over the last year, came out. "You can't make everything a pitched battle — too many casualties, and I'm afraid we're becoming one. Please, this is the perfect chance for us. Just walk away. Davies will find another horse to ride and another knight to joust at his windmills. They always do. You're just a cog in the machine."

"Bastard. I thought you cared about what I do."

"I do, just not who you do it for. Bradley Davies has been using you and you're so involved in fighting the battles that you can't see it. He's winning the war. There are other lawyers." He regretted that the minute it came out of his mouth.

"At least I'm involved in *something*."

He tried to let that pass, but was too far gone. "The two of us can't fix this. It's bigger than us." He regretted it the minute it came out of his mouth, but was too proud to back down.

"Damn right the two of us are done. I'll do it myself." She

stormed out.

Mac stood, stunned. He thought about going after her, but knew better. If she was going to calm down and see this clearly, she needed to do it by herself. He went back to the boat and got the box of supplies they had brought, took them upstairs, and laid them out on the counter. She was still nowhere in sight, but she couldn't have gone anywhere. He just needed to give her some time. There was no quick reconciliation for this one — she'd have to come around, one way or another, on her own.

He tore a sheet of paper out of a notebook and started to write.

When he was done, he left the note on the table and headed back to the boat. Maybe it was better to clean up the mess at home without her, anyway. She had her phone if she wanted to talk. He'd come back out in the morning and patch things up.

Chapter 23

Cesar checked the weapons as he loaded them into his truck. Two rifles, a shotgun, and a couple of handguns slid under the backseat. Then, satisfied he was ready for anything, he called to Jose.

"What's up?"

"Those gringos switched the stuff on us. Now those sand heads are all hot, and Diego needs to make them happy. *Es un loco mundo, amigo*." Diego had been clear about working with Ibrahim.

The terrorist limped out of the house as Cesar pulled to the curb. "You had better have a plan my friend."

"Let's drop the 'friend' shit. We're here to make our bosses happy. That's it." Cesar said.

"My boss, as you say, is Allah. I will succeed."

Silence prevailed as the truck made its way toward Marathon. Cesar was determined to end this tonight. While he was at it, he'd check and see whether the other gringo had come up with his money. He'd put that on the back burner after killing the hostages — pretty hard to make a trade when you had nothing to trade with. But if there was a chance he could get the hundred large, it would sure make the conversation with Diego easier.

They drove in silence, Cesar intentionally keeping Ibrahim in the dark. He liked to work alone and the thought of sharing his plans with an outsider angered him. The truck pulled into Mac's driveway and stopped next to a pickup.

"Stay here and watch the front." Cesar told Ibrahim as he moved carefully around back with Jose. They took turns leading and covering each other, not knowing whose pickup was parked or what to expect. They reached the back and moved up the stairs to the deck outside Mac's bedroom. He didn't notice the reflection in the glass of an empty seawall as he picked the lock on the sliding glass door. He sent Jose in first, scanning the back area before entering himself. Once in he used the flashlight mounted on his AK-47 to search the area. It was empty. The men moved downstairs. Blood congealed in pools where the victims had fallen, smudge marks showing where he had dragged the bodies out toward the water. Satisfied the house was empty, he sent Jose to get Ibrahim and settled in to wait. He was a patient man when he was stalking prey. Sooner or later the occupant would return. All his instincts pointed to the material being here.

* * *

Trufante was restless. Sue had the night shift, leaving him alone in her apartment, and he was both tired and wired, the pain killers mellowing him at the same time as the antibiotics and pain set him on edge. Sue had told him this might happen, not having the selection of antibiotics she had wanted, but hadn't told him what to do about it. He paced the apartment, flipping channels on the TV, and finally he gave up, showered, and left. She was going to be mad … if she found out. But the walls were seriously closing in on him.

Hoping alcohol would set him right, he took his regular seat at the bar, doing his best to keep his bandaged finger out of sight. Annie came over with a beer, leaned down, and pecked his offered cheek. A long deep drag on the beer, and he began to feel better. The bar was busy, thankfully, and the lack of his usual conversation went unnoticed. Two beers later, he was starting to level off. Maybe even feeling good, the alcohol doing its dance with the pain killers.

He hardly noticed when Heather entered.

She came right toward him, a tired-looking man following in

her wake, with determination on his face. He knew her by sight, had spoken with her once or twice, but she was more the kind of friend you nodded and smiled at. He gave her his trademark smile and hoped she would move past him, not really sure how well words would come out of his mouth in his present state. But she didn't veer away. Instead, she came right at him.

"Tru, I've got some questions for you. Could we go outside and have a chat?" She had no authority to question him, but was making herself friendly, obviously hoping that he'd play nice.

"Well sure, little lady," he said, grateful his mouth could still produce words.

He signaled for Annie to put his tab on hold and moved toward the door. Heather had to grab his arm when he tripped on the foot rail. She tightened her grasp as he stumbled again, guiding him through the door. Once outside, she parked him on a bench and sat next to him, making it less confrontational. The guy stood within hearing range.

"You want to tell me what happened to your hand?" she started.

"Oh this?" He held up his hand. "Just a little accident. I'm all good." Even in his present state he knew better than to tell the police anything.

"Well, we got a witness that puts you at a crime scene. A murder, actually. Can you tell me where you were last night?"

Trufante sobered slightly at that, and looked at the guy in the shadows. It took his scrambled brain a few seconds to realize that he knew the guy — one of the men from the house the night before. Shit.

"Might have been in some trouble," he answered slowly, shrugging. "I was kidnapped and dragged along. Been recuperating, else I would have come in and talked to y'all. I was planning on visiting tomorrow, telling you what I remember."

"Well, why don't we have that talk now." She took a small recorder from her purse and he nodded, accepting it.

"How 'bout we go back inside? I could use another beer. A lot more comfortable in there," he noted quietly. "This ain't gonna be a pretty story."

* * *

Heather knew she had to walk a line between what she could request of him and what she could demand. She followed along and went inside. They found a table in a quiet corner and she ordered him a beer. Anything, as long as he talked. She watched him as he sipped his beer and smiled, but she didn't have to look too closely to see him wobbling in his chair. Maybe a hospital would have been a better place to talk.

"You sure you're okay? We could take you over to the hospital and have them look at you."

"I'm good." He looked at his wrist, where his watch would have been if he'd remembered to put it on, and sighed. "Didn't he tell you what happened?" he asked, looking at Jeff.

"We know what happened in the house, how the drugs were found, and about Cesar taking the women."

Trufante looked like he was going to fall over. "You mean you don't know?" he gasped.

"Know what?"

"Well ..." He tipped off his chair and fell before he could complete the thought. His head hit the floor and bounced several inches before coming to rest.

Heather was immediately on him. He was out cold. She quickly examined him, and found his vitals steady, no evidence of a head injury. In fact, he just looked like a sleeping baby.

"Crap. Help me get him out of here. We should have taken him to the hospital as soon as I saw him."

Heather's mind was racing as they each grabbed an arm and walked him out of the bar.

Chapter 24

Mel wrote late into the night. It was cathartic and calmed her swirling mind. After the fight with Mac, she'd gone on a rampage, first cleaning the house, then burning her body with pushups and squats. She even tried to go for a swim to blunt the pain. And she hated to swim.

In the end, she wrote it all out. Her entire case, in longhand. The entire incident where Jim Gillum and the Navy had spied on her and Mac. And everything that followed. It took pages — mostly lists of reasons that drones had to be regulated now, not after they were in use. This was really the crux of the issue for her. Drone use was inevitable. The hardware and software had already been developed to fight terrorists. It was just a matter of time until they were crisscrossing the skies. Her concern was that they not be used against innocent citizens. As she wrote, though, she began to feel her quest was hopeless. She looked down at the cup of coffee she had brewed, thinking. It wasn't so much that she couldn't win, she was starting to doubt if she had the energy and resolve to fight the battle.

She'd had an idea brewing for the last year. It kept floating around in her head, surfacing whenever conflict arose. The concept was still fuzzy, so she started to write again, hoping she could finally define her thoughts. It was becoming harder to fight her cases. Battle lines, once clearly drawn, were now fuzzy. Her opponents had hidden agendas. Even her supposed allies, like Patel, had their own agendas. She'd always believed the law was defined by the constitution and should be argued by the merits of a case -- not it's blowback or affect on another case that may be won or lost based on this one. That was politics -- not law.

Then there was the general state of sanity. If you looked through someone, really got down to their motivations, you found that they were only motivated by a few things. Money was the usual culprit. Follow the money, and it usually led to the truth, and underlying motivation. Next were the genuine do-gooders. They truly wanted change for the sake of improving people's lot in life. The thing they didn't understand was that their agenda could have unintended consequences. They couldn't see past their initial goal, and really analyze a situation. Last were the people who had an agenda to make everyone live by their point of view. This last group had surrounded her for the last ten years, and during that time she'd come to realize that they were actually insane.

Maybe Mac was right. It was a losing battle. Her latest fight against the use of drones showed all this. Advocates for either side were hysterical in their support of their cause. These groups were as polarized as the zealots they sought to find with the drone programs. This made for an unwinnable situation. The government was too big, had too many branches, most not knowing what the other was doing. They had the press in their pockets. Then there were private contractors working for the government with their own set of rules. How could one issue take all that on, make it into the national spotlight and last more than one twenty-four-hour news cycle? The founding fathers, who she had come to respect more and more as time passed, used to deliberate and write things down. This was a stage of analysis and discussion that allowed time to pass, not the hurry up and get in front of a microphone before people forget who you are, which was the culture of politics today.

The edge had worn off by the time she finished writing. The room was in shadows, illuminated only by the gas lamp on the table. Her rage spent, she started to tear up as she looked around the room at her father's life. Every book and picture reminded her of good times or bad. Their relationship had been special through her first year of college. He'd raised her alone, her mother passing when she was in middle school. She admitted to herself reluctantly that he'd done a good job. She glanced around the room surprised to see her certificate from The University of Virginia. Going to the school had filled the void from being raised in the Keys, but had caused a rift between them. She had decided quickly, against her father's wishes, to get a law degree. As the years passed, she'd visited him less and hung out with her law friends more, their world views diverging, as generations often do. She had blamed it on his stubbornness, but realized later that stubbornness was a family trait, and she was just as guilty.

And now Mac. The lunkheaded conundrum she called him. Part hardcore Marine and part monk. The guy who could talk to Trufante in his Cajun slang, and turn around and quote Seneca about stoic values. She knew she had a way of intimidating men, but he was unusual. He would hear her out, not take her crap, and even give a healthy dose back to her.

She walked back to the shelves and looked at a picture of Mac and her dad some twenty years earlier, standing on a bridge piling next to a stack of books on Mayan civilization. She knew something was changing deep within her. She knew Mac had overreacted earlier, but she had pushed his buttons. He was the guy she truly wanted.

She fell on the couch and wept, the isolation here forcing her to reconcile with her demons. Her phone had died hours earlier, with no chargers out here. She turned the 12-volt VHF radio on for some background noise, and turned the squelch down, the static soothing her. Then she cried herself to sleep.

* * *

Mac eased the boat to the dock, skillfully judging the wind and tide, and using both to set the boat in place. He jumped out to tie the bow off before the wind got a hold of it. When he turned to go for the stern line, he found a gun to his head.

"Jose, tie off the boat. You," a hand pushed Mac toward the house, "we need to have a talk." Mac felt the pressure of the barrel on the back of his head as he was pushed towards the house.

They entered the building and moved towards the office, Jose came in behind them.

"Tie him up." The man pointed to the office chair. He kept the gun on Mac as Jose secured him.

He struggled against the restraints, watching as the man started to search the safe. "You got what you came for last night," Mac said.

"No, actually we didn't." The drug runner jabbed a finger in his face. "The material was switched. Didn't think I'd figure it out so quickly, did you?" He took a revolver out and spun the empty chamber. "You know, it's not really a gun if it's not loaded." He removed a box of bullets from the safe and loaded the gun, then spun the chamber again.

"Now, it's a gun." He held the gun to Mac's head. "Why don't you tell me where the right material is?"

"I don't know what you're talking about. My friend asked me to keep the box for him. I just put it in the safe. That's all."

"Your friend, the Cajun with the large smile? He's not smart enough to do that kind of switch." He waved the gun toward the shop. "You, on the other hand, look like you could easily accomplish the task."

Mac was at a loss now. He was about to deny it further when Cesar rammed the gun into his temple, knocking him unconscious.

* * *

Ibrahim walked in the door. He looked at Mac. Cesar had finished with the safe and was now rummaging through the office.

"You'll never find it in this mess. Let me question him," Ibrahim said.

"Suit yourself." He moved into the workshop and started digging through the piles of tools and gear.

Ibrahim went out to gather supplies. He found an empty bucket and filled it with water. Half was tossed on the unconscious man. He waited as he came to.

"Tell me where the material is, infidel,"

Mac's voice was slow, "I don't know what you're talking about. I told the other guy that I was just holding the box for a friend. I don't even know what's in it."

Then the drug runner was back. "Trufante ratted you out the moment the first drop of blood spurted from his finger. Maybe the same should happen to you."

"I can't tell you what I don't know."

"You keep looking." Ibrahim spotted a marine battery on the floor. "I will make him talk."

The terrorist found two wires and attached them to the battery. "Put his feet in the bucket."

Cesar complied.

"Now, before I have to hurt you, you will tell me."

Silence greeted the question. Sparks flew as Ibrahim grabbed the terminals and brushed them together. Satisfied he attached a clip to each earlobe and watched Mac writhe in pain.

Chapter 25

Sweat dripped from Mel's brow as she yanked the cord again. Nothing. She massaged her arm, tired from the exertion and sore from the thousand pushups she thought she'd done the day before. She'd been at it for a half-hour now, getting more frustrated with each failed pull. She'd moved Wood's old skiff out of the mangroves, where he had fashioned a camouflaged shelter for it. Now the eighteen-foot aluminum hull sat in the water, bow resting on the sand, but it wasn't going to do her any good if she didn't get it started.

Mel was no mechanic, but she'd grown up around outboards, and had no confidence that this one would start. The carburetor was sure to be gunked up from the old gas, and that was probably the least of it. Motors ran when you used them. Let them sit for a year and forget it.

She'd been up since dawn, after a restless night spent sleeping in short spells, broken by reenactments in her head of how the fight with Mac could have gone differently. She'd tried him on the VHF radio, knowing it was kind of a long shot, and her phone was dead. The solar system worked well, but she had no cable to charge it. Feeling isolated, she'd checked the horizon every few minutes, not really expecting to see the hull of Mac's boat appear, but hoping it would anyway. It would be afternoon at least before he came looking for her; knowing how long it took her to cool down was one of his attributes, although not convenient now.

Waiting wasn't in her genes, but the skiff wasn't going to start. She tied the boat off, too tired to pull it out of the water, and noticed an old canoe pushed back into the mangroves. The water in the bottom had turned brown from the decayed mangrove branches, mosquitoes hatching on its surface. Spider webs clung to every possible attachment. She was able to pull it out, but it held too much water for her to flip it.

Faced with the choice of cleaning the canoe or cleaning the carburetor, she chose the latter. She didn't dread the paddle as much as she feared hitting a wave and swamping the canoe. She released the cowling from the engine and removed the cover. The carburetor was not immediately visible so she followed the fuel line to reveal it's location. It took several trips back to the shed to accumulate the tools she needed to remove the fuel lines and choke cable from the carburetor. Once everything was disconnected she went to work on the screws holding it in place.

Now for the hard part. She took the carb to the shed and cleared room on the workbench, leaving the door open to allow more light to enter. The 12-volt fan did little to cool her off as she began to disassemble the unit. A dog eared manual, pages splayed from humidity sat open on the workbench. It'd been a long time since she'd watched her dad do this. She followed the cryptic instructions wishing she had her phone so she could take pictures as she went. Taking it apart would be easy - putting it back together was the real challenge.

Once she had disassembled the unit she set the parts to soak in an old can of cleaner that she hoped was still good. Strangely satisfied with the work — actually using her hands to do something — she started to straighten out the shed while she waited. Patience was never her strong point, but she waited what she thought was an hour before reassembling the components.

She took the carburetor back to the boat and started to reinstall it. The job complete she set the cowling back on the motor and secured it. Fuel line connected she squeezed the primer ball until it was full. She pulled the cord and nothing happened. Two more pulls and a small cloud of smoke erupted from the exhaust.

Another squeeze on the primer ball and she pulled again. This time it kicked to life. The motor evened out as she cycled the fuel, revving first and then letting it idle. Satisfied the motor was not going to stall she untied the line from the piling and hopped in the boat. She sat at the stern, holding the steering arm in her hand. A quick turn on the throttle and the boat moved off over the flats.

Chapter 26

Jules was confused. This didn't seem like a traditional kidnapping. "Strange that there hasn't been a call about the women. He said twenty-four hours. Sounds like something more is going on here and Sleeping Beauty has the answers we need," she said softly to Heather. They sat next to the hospital bed, waiting for Trufante to wake. He'd been unconscious since Heather had brought him in, and now lay on his back, IV in his arm, and the monitor on the other side of the bed beeping regularly, indicating he was still alive at least.

The doctors had assured them that it looked worse than it actually was.

"Can't they give him something to wake him up so we can talk to him?" Heather asked.

"I was thinking about giving him 'til morning. We need to get a court order to make a doctor do that, anyway. I've already started the paperwork for that — just need a judge to sign it."

Sue came in the room, chart in hand. She checked Trufante's vitals and added a syringe full of medicine to the IV.

"I might be able to help you," she said, overhearing their conversation. "Idiot here is, I guess, my boyfriend. I don't think he did anything wrong — came over last night and I bandaged him up and gave him some antibiotics. I told him to stay put, but he must have gone out when I left for work."

"We'd appreciate any help you can give us. I won't say anything to the hospital," Jules said.

"I appreciate that. I'm getting tired of sticking my neck out for him." She looked fatigued as well. "He must have had some pain killers before I got a hold of him, because he wasn't very coherent. Couldn't tell me much of anything, really. Mac Travis might be your best bet. I don't know how he's involved, but he dropped our boy here off with me, so I'm guessing he knows what happened."

"I know Mac," Jules said, wondering if this was Groundhog Day. The two men seemed to be connected at the hip when it came to trouble. "Here's my cell. Can you call me when he comes to?" She handed Sue her card.

"Sure, after I beat the crap out of him."

* * *

Mac slumped in the chair, unconscious. Water was pooled on the concrete floor around the bucket. His feet jerked again splashing more water onto the floor as Cesar applied the ends of the wire to his nipples. His body slumped again.

"Enough!" Ibrahim yelled. "We need him alive!"

"He's still breathing." Cesar went for the wires again, clearly enjoying himself. "This'll wake him up."

Ibrahim grabbed him as he was about to apply the wires, but Cesar shook him off, throwing him to the floor.

"We need answers. If I have to tell my contact in Mexico that you have been uncooperative, I'm sure he will show you the same treatment."

Cesar paused, wires in hand. The retribution Diego would exact if Travis was pushed too far and could not reveal the location of the material was enough to stop him. He set down the wires. "Maybe a change of scenery will help. He must have seen what we did to his friend's finger. I can take him to the bait shack. Show him the grinder. Grind off a finger or two. That'll jog his memory."

"You think this was not enough?" Ibrahim said. "We can try, but if you kill him....." he paused, "Where is this chum shack? Is the location secure?"

"*Si*. It is almost dawn, and the fisherman will be heading out soon. We can have the morning there with no one to bother us. That should be enough time to get what we need from him. His friend proved to be very cooperative when we introduced him to the machine."

"Very well. We can't stay here."

* * *

The black truck pulled onto US1, tires screeching as it ignored the stop sign.

"Those guys are lucky they didn't get a ticket," Jules said as she turned into Mac's street. She pulled into the driveway, and noted that the house was dark. "Stay here, I'll check it out."

She released the clip on her holster and placed her hand on her weapon. Slowly she walked the path, her head rotating left and right. She reached the door. No one answered after repeated knocks, so she moved toward the back of the house, where she tried the rollup door, only to discover that it was locked. Without reasonable cause, she couldn't enter the house. It was entirely possible that Mac was asleep upstairs and hadn't heard the door.

But she didn't think he was.

She went up the back stairs and knocked again. As she turned to leave, she noticed a dark stain on the concrete walk below, lit by the light from a window.

She motioned Heather over, indicating the stain. "Can you test that for blood?"

"I don't have my kit." Heather paused for a moment, then grinned. "Do you just need to know if it's blood or not?"

"I can't go in without probable cause. If that's blood, it's enough. Gives me a reason to get in there."

"Got a first aid kit?"

Jules ran back to the SUV and dug through the back and retrieved a first aid kit. She ran back around and handed it to

Heather. "Here you go."

"Cool. If there's some hydrogen peroxide in here, we can use that to test. It's not bulletproof, though."

Jules laughed. "Honey, I just need an excuse. And a quick one."

The stain boiled when Heather splashed peroxide on it. Seconds later, it turned pink. Heather looked up, eyes glowing. "Well, we've ruined it as evidence, but it's definitely blood. I'd bet on it."

Jules nodded once. "If there's blood out here, there's blood inside, and that's all the evidence I'll need. Go back to the car and call for backup. I'm going in."

Heather ran back toward the patrol car, as Jules climbed the stairs, smashed a pane of glass with the butt of her gun and reached in to unlock the door. She ducked in, and a moment later Heather joined her.

They took in the scene one piece at a time. The blood stains from the walk extended into the building and gathered in two pools, still wet, where it looked like someone had been shot. Although there was no blood in the office, the water bucket, battery, and wire brought up memories of old spy movies. She was horrified that another murder had occurred on her watch.

She turned to Heather. "Call one of the deputies and have them bring whatever you need. And I mean whatever you need. Screw the budget, we need to figure this out now." Her first thought was that the blood was from Mac.

Chapter 27

Heather was working the crime scene, a deputy helping her out and keeping watch in case anyone returned. She'd already taken blood samples from the two pools on the deck. No bodies had been discovered, so the coroner hadn't been called, but that didn't mean there wasn't something here. She assumed from the pools of blood that two people had been killed, their bodies moved. She asked the deputy to open the overhead door and they followed the blood stains out over the deck, to the seawall.

"Looks like they dumped the bodies in here. Can you call in and get us a diver?"

"That would be me. I've got my stuff in the truck."

"Awesome."

"Yeah, dead bodies, awesome."

"That's not what I meant. I'm going to call Jules while you get ready."

The deputy geared up, took a giant step off the seawall, and splashed into the murky water. Heather stood above him, watching his light move back and forth and holding her breath. Three dead bodies, all of them tourists, with one local missing and another in the hospital. This was getting weirder by the second. Suddenly a red inflatable float broke the surface. She had her phone in her hand, ready to make the call. The number was already on her screen when she hit *dial*, calling the coroner. The float could only mean the diver had found a body.

The bubble trail moved closer to the seawall and the diver broke the surface. "Looks like your bodies are down here. I found one already. Going down to look for the second."

She nodded. "Got it. How do we do this?"

"I'm going down to look for the other body. Then we wait for instruction from the coroner before I can move them. We're on standby for a few." He released the air from his BC and disappeared below the surface.

Heather watched the light and followed the bubbles for a few minutes before the next float popped to the surface.

* * *

Cesar dragged Mac into the bait shack, where a man with a rubber apron and gloves was grinding chum. He smiled, showing a gold tooth, when they entered, more enthusiastic about the disruption than was entirely appropriate. Mac, more conscious than he let on, let the drug lord drag him, hoping Cesar would let his guard down. His optimism waned when the door slammed.

"Cesar, you've brought more for the bait?" the man asked in Spanish.

"*Si,*" he let go of Mac and watched him fall to the ground.

He slit his eyes and looked around the room for a weapon while still trying to appear unconscious. He needed to act fast.

Cesar saw him move. "You saw your friend, the Cajun. We'll do the same to you," he snarled.

Mac gasped, but stuck to his story. "What do you want from me? I just put the thing in the safe."

"Do not take me for a fool. You're the only one that could have done this."

Mac could smell the fish oil on the breath of the man with the apron as he inched closer, but Cesar held up his hand.

"Not yet, my friend. This one is different than the other." The man went back to the chum table. "So, you see, I am not unreasonable. But you need to help me here."

"Alright, you want to talk? Why the hell are you working with terrorists that want to bomb us? You may be loyal to wherever you came from, but terrorism is bad for business. You think things are hard for you now, what happens after another attack? No more burner phones, more surveillance, drones? Your business will suffer." He tried to feed doubt to the drug dealer. "Maybe you should tell that to your bosses. Your people need to plan better."

The door opened interrupting them. "Do you have my answers yet?" Ibrahim walked into the room.

"We're still talking." Cesar moved toward the terrorist and Mac suppressed a grin. He *had* been listening, then. "Just for my curiosity, what are you planning on doing with the material when we retrieve it?"

"That is between the faithful and Allah."

Cesar got toe to toe with him, "Well, you tell Allah that this faithful servant is going to need some information. Maybe Allah would be unwise to use this here."

"No, not here."

"You know you can't fly with it. You're going to have to drive whatever bomb you build somewhere. And I bet it's close. Why would you risk transporting something like that? If it was me, I'd build it and blow it up right here," Mac said.

Cesar looked closely at him, considering, and then nodded. "Yes, my friend," he said, turning to look at the other man. "Tell me your plans."

"He's just going to lie. How much of your product goes through Miami? I know you sell some here, but this is too small a market. And Miami is the closest big city. For both of you."

"This is not yours to decide. I will call your patron. He will tell you what to do," Ibrahim snapped.

"Don't you worry, *terrorista*, I will recover the material. What I do with it after is another matter." He turned away from Ibrahim and went to Mac. A felt bag appeared from his pocket. Gold shined in the light as he pulled something out. "Maybe we need to talk about this as well." He held the gold sea serpent in front of Mac's face.

"That is of no interest to me. If you are not willing to do what is necessary to find the material, I will do it myself," Ibrahim said.

Without warning, Cesar grabbed the Arab's head and slammed him down against his knee. Ibrahim fell to the floor, unconscious.

"Now, tell me about this."

"What's there to tell? I bought it."

"You could not buy this. It is a Mayan artifact. They're not available anywhere but the black market, and I do not see you paying black market prices." He turned to the man with the apron, nodding at him to take over the interrogation. "*Mi amigo*, he is yours. I want answers."

* * *

Jules pulled back into Mac's driveway and watched as the first body was loaded into the coroner's van. Murder was rare here, and three in the last two days was not good for business. Although most crimes were committed by people passing through — crimes she couldn't really control — it was still a matter of pride that Marathon was a safe place. She got out of the car and entered the house, carefully lifting the crime scene tape as she walked in. Temporary lights lit the space, numbered markers littered the floor. She smiled at Heather and walked around back. It wasn't her place to interfere with the crime scene work. She would wait for them to finish, review the evidence, and go find the killer. She'd put a BOLO alert out for Mac, now that the bodies had been identified as women. Her instincts told her that he was not capable of this, but he was missing all the same. She had a feeling he was out trying to fix this himself. It wouldn't be the first time.

She sat at the back table and checked her phone, already knowing that she needed to call Jeff and break the news to him.

Not able to put it off anymore, she selected the second 813 area code number from her call log and hit *dial*.

He answered, sounding anxious. "Yes?"

"Jeff, Sheriff Whitman here. You okay?"

"Yeah, just nervous. That guy hasn't called yet. I'm getting scared."

"Where are you? We need to talk."

"Why, what's happened?"

"It can wait. Tell me where you are."

"At the hospital."

* * *

He was sitting erect in his chair, alone in the fourth floor lobby. She went up to the window that looked into the hospital room and stared at Trufante, still unconscious with what she took for a smile on his face. She'd wipe that off as soon as he came to. The asshole should have come to her immediately, rather than waiting. He might have saved some lives if he had. Shaking her head, she went to Jeff and placed a sympathetic hand on his shoulder.

"I'm so sorry, Jeff, there's no easy way to do this. We found your wife's body an hour ago."

He stared into space, shocked. Then he exploded with rage. "How could you let that happen? I thought you were on top of this!"

"I'm truly sorry, but it looks like she was killed before we got involved. Probably the night you went to Tampa. There's another body with her — a woman. I know this is hard, but I need you to identify them."

She waited patiently while he got over the initial response and composed himself.

"I need some time alone. Just write down where I need to go. I'll be there."

"It's no problem to take you." She couldn't remand him, but

127

didn't want to let him out of her sight.

He was silent for a long minute. "No, I've had enough police for the day. I'll take a cab. Just want to be alone for a few minutes."

"Okay, but we need you for this."

"Right."

* * *

Jeff waited until the elevator doors closed behind her. Then he pulled out his phone and dialed.

"Pete here. What's up?"

"The bastard killed them. The drug guy."

"Who are you talking about?"

"The guy that came to the house the other night. Killed Dan on the spot. Told me I had twenty-four hours to get some cash, and took the women. Then he killed them...."

"Oh my God. I'm so sorry. Where are you?"

"Hospital. It's a long story."

"Meet me outside. I'll be there in five. I think we'd better talk."

Chapter 28

Mel tentatively pulled up to the dock. Crime tape circled around the house and there were several people visible inside the rollup door. She thought about turning around and getting out of there after seeing the house converted to a crime scene. In the end, her sense of duty got the best of her. She tied the bow off and jumped onto the dock, then approached the first deputy she saw.

"Who's in charge here?" she asked.

"And you are?" He looked her up and down, and she realized that she hadn't seen herself in a mirror in a day. Grease, dirt, and sweat covered her skin and she probably had tear marks down her face.

"Melanie Woodson. I'm staying here." She had just started to feel comfortable here and now crime scene tape denied access to the house.

"I'm the lead officer here. Can you tell me what happened?"

"I haven't been here in a couple of days. Is Mac alright? Is he here?"

"He's missing. So, you are telling me you know nothing about this?"

"No, I got drunk the other night and we got in a fight." She abbreviated the truth.

"When was that?"

"Six or so, the night before last."

"And you just took off?"

Not wanting to be caught in an outright lie, she dodged the

question. "What's going on here? I need to charge my phone. Can I get my charger, at least?"

"As long as it's upstairs. Everything down here is a crime scene."

She headed up the outside stairs. "I'll need a statement.," he called after her, staring up at her from the bottom step.

"No problem, just give me a few minutes." She entered the sliding glass door leading to the bedroom, thankful the crime scene had not extended here. She sat on the edge of the bed, head in hands. The grime and grit were like sandpaper, her hair oily.

The dirt swirled down the drain, as she wished the past few days would disappear with it. She stood under the stream of hot water from the shower deep in thought. Where was Mac? Jules was a childhood friend and she trusted her. Maybe the best thing was to find her and lay out everything that had happened. Her brain went into lawyer mode, trying to decide if Mac had done anything illegal, or just been an idiot. She smiled, remembering her dad's line - *rule #1 - boys are idiots.* The worst she could think of was obstructing justice. She was confident Jules would drop whatever charges might be pending in exchange for any information she had. Galvanized by her decision, she turned the water to cold. The hot water had been lulling her to sleep.

She stepped out of the shower and had just changed when she heard a knock on the door.

"Mel? You in there?"

"Yeah, I'll be right out."

Mel left the room and met Jules in the hall. She moved forward and hugged her old friend. "Mel, you know what happened here?" There was a built-in level of intimacy between the two women, who had a long history together, growing up here.

"I hate to admit it, but I was drunk that night. I passed out, and the next thing I know Mac had us on the boat. I'm really sorry."

"No worries, girl. Where is he?"

"Wish I knew. We got in a fight. I just got back from dad's place." She paused. "Listen, Mac told me some stuff. I know he could be in some trouble here - not for what's downstairs. Maybe withholding information or something. I'll tell you what little I know if you promise not to charge him.

"Mac Travis, withholding information - like that's a new one. Sure, if that's all it is go ahead. But, if he's involved any other way I'm going to have to go after him," Jules said.

Mel relayed the conversation she'd had with Mac, trying to remember everything she could. "That's it. We went out to dad's yesterday and got in a fight. That's the last I saw him."

"Your dad. I haven't seen you since then. Really sorry about him. You know how much I liked him."

"Thanks. Anything else I can do for you? I've got a pile of messages, and I want to find Mac."

"No, you know the old line though: Don't leave town."

They hugged again as Jules left, leaving Mel alone with her phone.

When she dialed, Mac's number went straight to voicemail. She was getting worried. She went to the front window and saw his truck parked out front. More anxious now, she followed Jules down the stairs. "His truck and boat are both here, cell phone's going to voicemail. I'm worried something's happened to him."

"I put out a BOLO on him when we saw what happened here. Nothing yet," Jules said.

"I'm really worried. Whatever you find out, please let me know." She glanced around, jaw dropping, as she saw the scene for the first time. The crime scene seemed more vivid with the police tape, lights and numbered signs. "Please, find him."

A woman, bent over examining something, called Jules over. "There's something here that I couldn't place. There's blood here," she said, shining her light down and tracing a path from the front door to the office. "Look at the direction of the spots. Someone came *in* bleeding."

Mel and Jules stood side by side following the light. "Maybe Trufante," Jules said.

"That's what I was thinking. So, we have the blood trail, but look." She shined her light on what looked like mud, and looked up again. "I couldn't figure it out, but the smell got me." She bent down and scratched at the stain, picking up a piece and rubbing it back and forth between her latex-clad fingers. "It's fresh, too, look at the oil. It's chum. Don't know what it has to do with this, but I'd be looking for a bait grinder. Maybe Monster — they're the biggest bait outfit here."

Chapter 29

Jeff stood on the sidewalk in front of the hospital, his face tired and drawn. He didn't know what to think or how he should be reacting, but he felt angry.

Pete pulled up and stopped. Jeff got in but did not acknowledge him.

"Hey, bud, you all right?" Pete asked.

"You son of a bitch!" Jeff screamed. "My wife is gone because of you. Some great idea - get a Mexican drug dealer involved. Dammit." He moved towards Pete.

Pete shrunk back, "I know how you're feeling, but this isn't my fault. Dan was the one who insisted on keeping the stuff. You were right along with him. I wanted to dump it."

"Whatever." He slammed the dashboard with his fists. "I'm so freakin' mad. I know I shouldn't feel this way, but I want revenge. How do we find this son of a bitch?"

"Key West. I followed him. I know where he lives, but there's something else."

"What's that?" Jeff asked.

"There was a package inside the bundle that was different."

Jeff stared off into space. "So?"

"The guy, he took one package and met this Middle Eastern-looking guy in a park. He handed him the package and took off. I didn't know what else to do so I followed that guy, too."

"This has nothing to do with me. I just want the Mexican."

"Maybe we should just tell the authorities what I saw and get out of here before something bad happens."

"Like something worse is going to happen. My wife's dead.

How do you think that feels." He slammed the dashboard again. "You want to walk away from this with nothing to show for it? I don't. Screw the authorities. Even if they catch the guy, he'll probably walk."

"You're in some kind of shock. Think about it. We don't have the skill set to go after these guys. We don't even have a gun." Pete was scared by his friend's anger.

"I've got this in perspective."

"You've got revenge in your sights. I get that. We need to take what we have and go to the police," Pete pleaded.

"Okay, so maybe it's not all revenge." The adrenaline that had fired his earlier reaction seemed to be wearing off. "It's the same as why you followed the guy. I just have to see this through. We get some more information we can turn it over to the authorities. I promise. I need to do this."

"If I've got your word — no more drugs."

"Yeah."

They looked at each other, each evaluating the other's sincerity.

"What now?" Pete finally asked.

"That guy that was going to make the trade for us. He's in the hospital here." Jeff said. "He owes us."

* * *

Jules turned the lights off as she entered the driveway to Monster Bait, the wheels louder than she liked as they ran through the crushed coral of the driveway. Twilight had just faded into full on night, the moon not yet visible. At least they would have some cover when they went in.

She parked behind a stack of crab traps and turned to Mel, "I got a vest that'll fit you, but you gotta stay back. I'd have you stay here, but I think it's safer to have you with me."

Mel took the vest, put it over her head and strapped the velcro closures. "I'll stay back, don't worry about that."

"Keys are under the mat if something happens." Jules pulled

out her gun and started moving toward the only sign of life — a light shining through a window fifty yards away.

They moved closer using the shadows cast by the trap piles, carefully avoiding the buoys and line scattered on the road. When they were within a few feet, they stopped behind a stack of traps. Shadows were visible in the shack now. They couldn't tell how many, but it was more than one. Muffled voices whispered through the night. Jules pointed to Mel, motioning for her to wait, and moved toward the building. She could make out three figures now, but their voices were disguised by the sound of a machine. She stayed low, below the window, listening.

* * *

"Gringo," Cesar said, "I do not believe you. You're going to need to convince me, or I'll let my friend here make chum out of you."

Mac watched him as he glanced over at the man in the apron. "What's it going to take? I have no idea where they came from." He was getting desperate.

"Enough of this." Cesar nodded to the large man. "He's yours."

The man came toward Mac, grabbed his hand, and quickly locked out the wrist, putting enough pressure on the joint that Mac followed obediently. Mac could smell the fishy smell of the man's breath as they moved closer to the grinder. His hand and maybe more would be gone if he didn't act now. Feigning faint he pushed forward using a classic Aikido move to throw the other man off balance. As he tried to compensate he released the pressure on his wrist. Seeing the opening he executed a sweep kick, landing the man on the ground, but Cesar moved toward him, gun extended.

They were all startled as the door crashed open losing one of its hinges. All three men watched as Jules pulled back from her mule kick and spun into a shooting stance. "Police! Freeze!"

Cesar swung his gun from Mac to the door. Before he could

shoot, Jules fired wide as a warning before refocusing on his head. He was about to drop the gun when Jules hit the floor.

"You owe me one." Ibrahim dropped to a knee. He took the gun from Jules and handcuffed her with her own cuffs. Then he removed her belt, with the radio, cell phone and pepper spray. "Maybe now we can take care of what I need."

"We have leverage now." Cesar rose. "We keep the woman. Let him go. Mr Macho here will lead us right to it."

"Bad idea. I no longer trust you. What are you thinking, we can't just let him walk away."

"I'm thinking. That's what separates us," Cesar said. "Jose, follow him. Stay back and keep me updated on what he does. He knows we have her." A finger pointed at the sheriff. "He'll do the right thing. Here," he reached in his pocket and took out several phones and tossed Mac his phone, "Stay in touch."

Mac looked at Jules as she started to move on the floor. He glanced at the bait grinder knowing that she had saved him from it's whirling teeth. He nodded at her as she tried to focus on him, hoping she saw the determination in his eyes.

Chapter 30

Trufante was sitting up in bed a tray on the table in front of him. He was toying with the jello, giggling as it jiggled when the two men entered the room. He looked up, "Howdy, boys."

"Glad to see you're feeling better," Pete said sarcastically.

"Leave it to the doctors to get my meds dialed in for me. I'm feelin' fine." His fascination with the jello continued.

"Good, because we need your help," Jeff said. They had agreed that, if Trufante wouldn't cooperate, Jeff would play the bad guy.

"I ain't in no condition to help anyone right now." He wiggled his legs. "See that? I can't even feel them. You know that Pink Floyd song, *I Have Become Comfortably Numb*? Well, that's what I feel like." He started humming the tune.

Pete turned to Jeff. "He's worthless."

"Yeah, I guess we need to do this ourselves."

Trufante overheard them. He may have been drugged up, but he understood what they implied. "Alan *TRU*fante ain't worthless to no one. You tell me what you want done. I can operate in any condition. Just watch."

His feet hit the floor and he tried to stand, then swayed for a minute before gaining his equilibrium. He took a step but was restrained by the IV in his arm. "This part I may regret." He pulled the IV out and placed his bandaged finger over the exit hole to stem the bleeding. "We're off."

"Your off to see the wizard is where you're off to." Jeff looked at Pete. "He's no use to us." He started to leave.

137

"Y'all got no faith in my Cajun disposition. You just help me out of here. The drugs'll wear off sooner than later. Unfortunately."

"He's right," Pete said. "We get him out of here and sit on him a couple of hours, he'll sober up."

"What the hell. He does know all the players. Any trouble, we can ditch him." Jeff grabbed onto one of his arms and started walking him to the door. "Grab his clothes."

* * *

"He ought to be sober enough," Pete said. They sat in Trufante's apartment. Both men anxious.

They'd reached a decision while Trufante had nodded out that they would offer the drugs as bait, hoping that would entice him to cooperate.

Trufante had finally stopped humming *Comfortably Numb*, as he no longer felt the love an hour later. "All right. Let's get it on. This is as sober as I'm planning on gettin'," he mumbled.

"Okay, here's the deal. You help us recover the drugs and the box, and we'll cut you in for a third," Pete said. He was playing the good cop. If Trufante didn't cooperate, Jeff was ready to jump in with the bad cop routine.

"I could use some of that about now. A little bump would sure taste good." He licked his lips. "Yeah, that's all good." But about that box, no dice there."

"All or nothing."

"You boys know what's in that box?"

They shook their heads.

"Plutonium. Weapons-grade stuff."

"All the more reason to go after it," Pete said. "I saw the exchange, and I bet that guy's a terrorist. They could be building a bomb right now. Be a patriot."

"I want to remain a live patriot. Those are some seriously mean dudes you're messing with."

Jeff needed to get this moving. "All right, forget about the box. We just go for the drugs, then."

"Y'all got a plan?"

"We know where he lives. You're gonna walk right in and distract him. We'll sneak around back and take him from behind. Then we find the drugs and get out of there. Call the police to go get him and we'll be back here an hour later. "

"It's never that easy. Take it from me. I've stepped in enough crap in my life."

* * *

"Hey."

Mac jumped, but quickly regained his cool. He was walking away from the bait shack. "Mel?" His spirits lifted, but concern overtook him. "Stay back. Out of sight!" he whispered harshly.

"They can't hear us from here," Mel said as she followed his pace, keeping in the shadows of the trap piles.

"I'll bet they've got someone following me. Stay out of sight and keep your voice down." Mac said. "They let me go to retrieve the material."

"Where's Jules?" Mel asked.

"They've got her. That's why they let me go. They know I'll do whatever it takes to get her back."

"Crap. What do we do? She left the keys to the SUV under the mat. We can use that," she said.

"Okay, I'm gonna walk out of here. You stay here until you see the guy following me leave. I don't know if he'll be on foot or in a car. Once it's clear, go for the car and get out of here. I'll be walking north on US1 on the southbound side. That'll make it harder for him to follow. Just cruise by and open the door. Don't stop, just slow down a little and I'll get in." He paused, about to say something, but then moved on in silence, leaving her behind.

* * *

She stayed behind the trap pile, watching for the tail. A few minutes later the door to the shack opened and a man came out. He went down a side path towards a truck. Needing a better vantage point, she started climbing a trap pile, using the slats of the traps as hand and foot holds, trying to gain a better vantage point. They supported her small frame easily, without toppling over. She got to the top quickly, holding herself with her eyes just over the top of the last trap, hands and feet wedged into the slats. Mac was out on the street now. The truck was following him slowly, keeping far enough back that Mac might not have seen it, lights out and idling. The sound of the engine and wheels crunching the ground coral soon blended in with the other sounds of the night.

Her fingers were cramping when she descended the pile. The car was far enough away now that the driver wouldn't be able to see her in the blackness, even if he looked in his rearview mirror. Slowly, she moved for the police SUV and quietly let herself into the driver's side. Once there, she breathed deeply and reached for the keys. Her hand found nothing. She started to panic, her hand swiping around on the floorboard, but finally she found the keys. Looking around, she thought it was likely to be as safe as it was going to get.

It was now or never.

She started the car and shoved the handle into drive, then, not thinking of anything other than Mac, she peeled out and went for the road.

A gun shot rang out, causing her to swerve. Another bullet quickly followed, shattering the rear window. The back-up lights from the truck came toward her from the driveway, while the gunman closed on her rear. Boxed in by equipment and traps on both sides, she put her hands on the steering wheel, hoping they wouldn't just shoot her.

"Out of the car, *punta*." A dark guy opened the door,

grabbed her shoulder, and pulled her to the ground.

"Mac!" she screamed.

"It's no use. He's gone, but once he knows that you're my guest, he'll cooperate even more." He looked in the car, taking the keys and her cell phone.

They walked along the gravel path back towards the bait shack, the man behind her with the gun. The door opened revealing Jules pressed into the corner, the man with the apron leering at her, Ibrahim pointing her own gun at her.

"Mel. You okay? Sorry to get you in this," Jules said.

"It's okay," Mel said, not really feeling it. "We should be okay. They want Mac to do something for them, then they'll let us go."

"I wouldn't be so sure about that," Jules muttered.

"You two, smile." Cesar used Mel's phone to take a picture, then scrolled through the contacts and sent it to Mac as a text message. "That oughta get his attention.

Chapter 31

Mac was soaked from rain and sweat. A rain cloud had just dumped its contents on him — typical this time of year. The aftermath of these short storms gave a new definition to humid. His muscles kept cramping and spasming as if they remembered the shocks he had been tortured with. Fatigue overwhelmed him. He walked, facing the oncoming traffic. If Mel had gotten out of the lot okay, she should be pulling up anytime. All he wanted was to get her safe and disappear. Maybe go back out to Wood's place. Even if they could find him there, he would see them coming. The house offered a 360-degree view that went for miles. He walked closer to the street, wondering what was taking Mel so long. Suddenly Jules's SUV pulled up. Relieved, he ran to meet the car, reached out to open the door, and realized too late that it wasn't the right car. A boy and girl pointed at him, laughing, as they pulled away, leaving Mac in the street.

He sat on a nearby park bench, trying to recover his pride, and watched the traffic. Another spasm shook his body, leaving him spent. He leaned over from exhaustion, when his phone beeped, signaling a new text message. He pulled it from his pocket and opened the message to see a picture of Mel and Jules staring at him.

He got up and started walking, his fatigue replaced by rage.

* * *

Mac stood in front of the apartment door waiting. He could hear voices coming from inside and felt the presence of someone on the other side of the door staring through the peephole.

"You expecting anyone?" Mac heard a voice call out.

"I'm popular."

Mac banged harder. The door opened, he pushed Jeff aside and entered the apartment. Trufante started to get up, but couldn't find his legs.

"Who are these guys?" Mac snapped.

"These are the dudes that found the package," Trufante slurred.

Mac looked at them. "Should'a let it keep on going," he muttered, shaking his head.

He felt their eyes on him, standing in the small foyer, water puddling at his feet. Disgusted, he turned his gaze toward Trufante, ignoring the other men. "I'm gonna borrow a change of clothes, then we're gonna figure out how to undo this mess you started." He went to the bedroom, emerging minutes later dressed in a Bob Marley T-shirt and cargo shorts.

"What'cha have in mind?" Trufante asked.

"I've got no idea. They've got Mel and Jules. Even if we called the Feds, it might be too late as trigger happy as our boy is." He sat down at the table.

"If all they want is the box, couldn't we just give it back?" Pete asked.

"Sure, then they shoot us, and the girls. That box is the only reason any of us are still breathing."

"Shee-it," Trufante said. "We gotta set 'em up. Classic con, man. "Down in the Bayou, you got to fend for yourself."

Mac knew better, but had no other ideas. "Go ahead," he said.

"They know the stuff you swapped out is low grade, right? We need some of the good stuff. Give them a little sample, let'm test it. Then we bring 'em out in the open. Get the girls back."

"Keep going." A plan was forming in Mac's head.

* * *

Mel's phone vibrated on the stainless steel counter. "Looks

like someone wants you," Cesar said, picking up the phone. "One new email. Let's see what's up in this pretty lady's life." She watched him, feeling violated as he scanned through her phone. "Interesting. What do you know about lover boy and Mexico?"

"What are you talking about? Let me see that."

He tossed the phone to her. "I'm watching you."

She read the email. *It has come to our attention that one Mac Travis had been in electronic communication with an unknown party in the province of Tabasco, Mexico. The language is cryptic, but it can be assumed he is communicating about some kind of antiquities. Please explain this, it affects our case.* She pressed the button for more details, revealing the history of the message. It was forwarded from the NSA to Patel. She read it again, hoping it would make sense. "What does this have to do with anything?"

"Maybe I can help." Cesar tossed her the bag. "This was in his safe."

She opened it and took out the two gold pieces. They were ancient — two gold versions of a sea serpent, and she looked up, confused.

"Unfortunately, I can tell from the look on your face that you don't know anything about this. Very unfortunate." He extended his hand for the pieces. "Looks like Mr. Mac Travis is in more trouble than he thought."

"What are you talking about?" Mel asked.

Cesar started, "My people, the Chontal Mayans are descendants from the Olmec, a civilization long before the Aztecs and Mayan cultures. Our people are pure, untainted by Spanish blood. Those gold pieces belong to our tribe."

Chapter 32

Cesar was looking out the window at the yard. It had been deserted when they got here. Now it was starting to show activity, and that made him very nervous. Commercial fishing boats were pulling up to the dock to offload their catch. Wouldn't be long before the place was crawling with fishermen. "We need to get out of here."

"Where to?" Ibrahim asked.

"I've got an idea." Cesar opened the door and pushed Jules out. "Walk to the truck. Do nothing to attract attention or I'll put a bullet in your friend." He pushed the gun barrel into the small of Mel's back to prove his point, then turned to his henchman.

The group walked to the SUV and Cesar settled into the driver's seat, Jose rode shotgun, Ibrahim and the girls in back. He pulled out slowly onto the drive, and accelerated. They drove in silence, north on US1. He made a right at Publix and a left at the Sombrero Country Club. The turns started coming faster as he passed the Flamingo Key sign, checking his rearview mirror to make sure they weren't being followed.

Many houses were shuttered this time of year — a precaution against the coming hurricane season, their owners gone north for the summer. It was perfect. He pulled into the driveway of a large white stucco house with a garage — something that had increased the breadth of his search. Carports were common here, garages often converted to storerooms. He needed to keep the truck out of sight.

"Wait here with them." He went to the rear of the truck and opened the tonneau cover that hid and protected the contents.

Crowbar in hand, he closed the cover and went to the side of the house. A few minutes later, the garage door opened and he pulled the truck in. A quick check of the street and he pushed the button to lower the door.

He went in first, followed by the girls and Jose. The house was like a tomb, the only opening ... the shutter he had jimmied open at the laundry room door. He went to the thermostat and turned on the AC, then checked the refrigerator, took out four Cokes, and handed them around. The group assembled in the living room.

"I hope your boyfriend comes through for you." He took Mel's phone out and texted Mac to call when he was ready to make the exchange. "Make yourselves comfortable. We wait here until he calls." He turned on the TV, sat back in the recliner, and sipped his Coke.

* * *

Mac looked out the window of Trufante's apartment. The sky was a light grey with several dark spots where thunderheads were building. Early evening was an active time of day for the storms, nurtured by the heat of the day; the wind had picked up, maybe two to four-foot seas. Nothing bad, just a little bumpy for a night dive. But he didn't have a choice; he had to retrieve the package to make the trade. Although he didn't have any intention of handing over the material, he needed the bait.

Mac remained at the table; Pete sitting across from him. Trufante was entrenched on the couch. Jeff paced the room. Mac was laying out his plan, but obstacles arose at every turn.

"The problem is I've got no air. I used the last tank of Nitrox setting it down there." He needed the Nitrox mix to increase his bottom time. Regular air tanks would only allow a few minutes at depth. The enriched air allowed almost twice the bottom time.

"How deep do you have to go?" Jeff asked.

"It's eighty feet, and in the dark, it's gonna take a while to

146

find it."

"We've got a couple of tanks at the house. Plain air, though," Pete said.

"It'll have to do. You got gear? I'd rather not go by my place." Mac thought about the risks of the decreased bottom time using plain air. It was going to take him awhile to find the stash at night. Visibility during the day ranged from twenty to over a hundred feet. He could usually see the shapes of the coral heads rising from the bottom as he descended. At night, he might have five feet of visibility. He would have to descend to the bottom, find the ledge, and work from there. A night time decompression stop to allow the nitrogen to dissipate from his blood was dangerous as well. In his current condition he wanted to get in and out as soon as possible.

"We can set you up," Jeff said.

"What about your boat? We need that too. Get Trufante ready, we gotta go." Mac rose from the table, his legs shaky.

* * *

Mac scanned the water. He would have been more comfortable on his boat at night, especially a night as dark as this. He had spotlights, controlled from the wheelhouse and radar. The small boat had only the required navigation lights. He had kept the green and red lights on the bow on, but disabled the white anchor light to help their night vision. The moon had not risen and the tide was out, making the navigable portion of the channel smaller. Conditions could not get any worse to navigate the narrow pass. They moved slowly through Sister's Creek Channel. Jeff stood in the bow, shining a flashlight on the markers, which were otherwise invisible.

"Watch that one." Mac pointed to the red marker on their left. "Big rock right on the other side of it. Seen a bunch of tourists try and cut that corner too hard in a rush to get out there, and tear the lower units off. Don't want to be another Captain Crunch."

"How are you going to find the spot?" Pete asked.

Mac pulled out his cell phone. "Finally figured out a good use for this sucker." He opened the GPS app, scrolled through a couple of screens, and selected the waypoint labeled "Rock." The screen showed a compass needle pointing in the direction they needed to go, and Mac set the phone down on the dash in front of Pete.

"Just follow that. Take her easy and go wide around Sombrero. This dark, you won't see anything floating in the water." Thankfully, lobster and stone crab were both out of season. Those times of year, the water would be littered with trap lines and buoys — instant death for a propellor.

Jeff came back from the bow as the boat passed the red blinking light, the last marker before open water. In the distance, they could see the intermittent flashing of the light on Sombrero Key, marking the reef five miles out.

Chapter 33

The phone started to beep as it zeroed in on the waypoint. Mac looked around for something to mark the spot, but came up empty. He took the wheel from Pete and started circling, checking the depth finder as he went. Thoughts of Mel and Jules were pushed to the back of his mind as he focussed on the task at hand. The adrenaline of the coming dive replaced the fatigue.

"This is hard enough in daylight. We need something to throw out and mark the spot."

Mac yelled at Trufante, "Wake up, sunshine. We need the chair cushion." Mac had handed the wheel back to Pete, and was stripping line off a fishing rod using his six foot wingspan to measure it. When he got to a hundred and fifty feet, he cut the line. There was little on the boat to work with and he had to improvise. The pocket of the BC yielded a five-pound weight, which he tied to one end of the line. "How much weight did you have in there?" he asked.

"There was only eight pounds of weight in there. You're bigger than me. How are you going to get down?" Jeff asked.

"It's going to be hard to get down and stay there without the weight." Usually a very efficient diver, his air supply lasted longer than the bottom time. But without the extra weight he would have to work harder and use more air. Running out of air was now added to his list of problems.

Trufante was moving now, slamming into the gunwales, unable to get his body synced with the rhythm of the seas. "Got any beer? My buzz is fading fast."

Pete nodded toward the cooler, but Mac cut him off. "Need him sober."

He tied the seat cushion to the other end of the line and waited for the GPS alarm to indicate that they were over the waypoint. It beeped and he tossed the weight, hoping the line wouldn't tangle as he hand-fed it. When he was done, the cushion bobbed on the waves, marking the spot.

"Stay with the cushion. If it moves - follow it." Mac said as he suited up. "I'll be on the other end."

He was in the water, flashlight in hand. He finned for the cushion, grabbed the line, and descended. It was pitch dark on the way down and looked like a disco ball spinning in a dark room as the light beam reflected off particles suspended in the water. The visibility ended at the range of the flashlight — maybe ten feet. Not great, but for a night dive you got what you got. Without the extra weight he fought to descend. The bottom came into focus as the light illuminated the coral and fish. He disregarded the scenery, double checked his air and started the timer on his watch.

The reef was more active at night. He ignored the lobsters bravely walking across the sandy bottom, seeking new homes, empowered by the night. An octopus floated by him, translucent in his light. In the limited visibility he was unable to find the landmark coral heads, he took forty-five frustrating minutes just to locate the rocks blocking the cavern. Now he was concerned about the time — already six minutes past the no-decompression limit, he calculated the stops he would have to make on the way up. Twenty feet for ten minutes, and then ten feet for another ten minutes. Nothing you wanted to do at night, especially without an anchor line to hold on to.

He shivered as he removed the BC and set it on the sand next to the opening. Regulator clamped in his teeth, he moved the rocks blocking the entrance and eased his way in. The light illuminated the coral, and the lead ball was visible where he'd left it. He grabbed for it, pulled out of the cavern and reattached his gear. Ball in hand he grabbed the weighted line and started to ascend. A quick glance at his gauges showed the air pressure well below 500 psi, deep in the red zone. As if on cue, the air came harder with each breath, until it stopped. He didn't need to look at his pressure gauge to know he was out of air. His depth gauge read sixty feet. At a second per foot, the fastest safe ascent, he would need to hold his breath for a minute to reach the surface safely. He kicked his fins, knowing he was going too fast. Ascending faster than your own bubbles was the first thing you learned not to do in your first open water class. But he had no choice. Better to add a few more minutes to his decompression time than to black out and drown.

He reached the boat and yelled for another tank. Changing tanks while in the water was risky, but he didn't have time to get on the boat, swap them and then get back in the water. He needed to start his decompression right now or risk the bends. The seas had increased in the short time he had been down, the wind picking up as darkness cooled the air. The boat bobbed up and down, making it difficult to communicate.

Hoping the men had understood what was needed, he blew into the purge valve on his BC. The BC inflated allowing him to bob on the surface. He turned onto his back and swam to the boat, giving directions as he closed the gap. Time was the enemy now, every second brought him closer to the bends.

"Hey, drop the anchor," he yelled. Two splashes within seconds indicated the anchor had been dropped and at the same time a tank splashed into the water next to him, a line attached to it. The lead ball still in his hand, so he tossed it onto the boat, grabbed the line, and tied it off to his inflated BC. Not wanting to waste the time to change tanks, one hand reached behind his head, unscrewed the first stage from the spent tank, and attached it to the new tank. Then, the full tank cradled in his arms, he turned the air valve on and let the air out of his BC. He sank into the darkness stopping at twenty feet, the line his only connection to the boat.

The boat bounced in the waves above him, pulling the line tight in his hand every time a wave hit. It felt like an hour, but his dive watch showed only ten of the twenty minutes he needed until he moved up the line for another twenty minutes at ten feet. As he hung there, the wave action increased. Another twenty minutes and he calculated he'd be okay. He shivered and settled in to wait. Exhaustion set in and his thoughts drifted to Mel.

He started to doze off on the line, but jerked awake when a large wave must have slammed the boat. The bow lifted in the air, pulling the line from his hand, and within moments it was out of his reach. He finned toward it, panicking at the sudden lack of connection, but couldn't reach it, the boat's bulk pushed by the wind and current, moving it faster than he could swim.

* * *

Trufante was the first to notice that the boat was moving. He'd sobered up enough to feel the hull turn sideways, parallel with the seas. An anchored boat would have it's bow pointed into them.

"Dude, check that anchor. That wave must have pulled it," he grumbled, already moving toward the line. If they moved too far, it would be trouble. Though he couldn't quite remember why.

Pete went forward and pulled the line Mac was holding. Instead of resistance, the line came in easily. "He's gone. What now?"

Trufante went to the helm and started the engine. "Pull those lines in quick! Mac should be around here somewhere, we have to find him. How long's he been in?"

No one answered and Trufante, suddenly sober, fumbled with Mac's phone, trying to get the GPS to start working again. "You guys keep a lookout for him or the cushion -- anything." He scanned the water ahead of them,desperate, wishing for more of a moon to penetrate the darkness.

* * *

Mac drifted in the current, the boat's lights fading in the swells. Even at the crest of a wave, he was unable to see it. He knew yelling would be futile, but he had to do something. His hands went for the BC, instinctually finding the left clip. But he came up empty, groaning. His own equipment had a signal whistle clipped to the left and a multi-tool to the right side. Both clips on the borrowed vest were empty. He got onto his back, the inflated BC keeping his head out of the water. With no need of the full tank, he jettisoned it and floated freely. No point carrying the extra weight.

He had to figure out a way out of this mess.

Trained as a commercial diver, instinct took over. He knew they would be searching for him, but doubted even a trained search and rescue operation would be able to find a lone diver in these kinds of seas at night. At least the commercial boats handed out glow sticks to attach to everyone's tanks. Shore was five miles away. The next closest structure was Sombrero Reef. He glanced over his right shoulder and saw the light blinking from the 142-foot tower. It looked to be less than a mile away, the seas running toward it. Accepting this as his best option, he rolled onto his stomach and took a quick compass heading. Once on his back he reversed the heading and started to kick, eyes focused on the compass.

Chapter 34

Cesar stood in the kitchen, Mel's phone in his hand, waiting for an answer from Mac. He had sent a picture of Mel and Jules as hostages. "Your boyfriend is late. Maybe I should get Jose to cut off your finger or something. I can take a picture and send it to him." He held the phone up. "Very good for business -- these things."

Jose took the cue and grabbed a knife from the counter and went toward her. Cesar smiled as the girls shrunk into each other on the couch.

"He had to go out to the reef and dive for it," Mel said.

He went to her and slapped her face. "Why did you not give me this information before?"

"Doesn't matter. He's getting it."

"I wish I could be sure of that."

"Call Trufante, then. I'd bet he's with him."

Cesar scrolled through her contact list and dialed the number. It started ringing and he hit the speaker button and placed the phone on the counter.

"Yo Yo Yo - You okay?" Trufante answered.

"This is not the lady. I think you know this voice, Cajun."

"What have you done with her?"

"Don't worry, she's fine. She's right here. Maybe if you cooperate, you'll get to see her again." He eyed the girls.

"Mac went after the box. We have it, but we lost him."

"What do you mean, you lost him?" Cesar yelled into the phone. Mel's head snapped toward him, fully alert now, and he listened as Trufante spoke.

"Screw him. You are going to bring the box and meet me at

the bait shack in an hour. If you are late I may have to take some more pictures."

* * *

"We got complications," Trufante said.

"This is going to get worse?"

"We don't have a chance in hell of finding Mac out here, but he's got the skills to deal with this. The dude says he's going to kill the girls if we don't meet him in an hour."

"Fine. Call the Coast Guard and let them do their job," Jeff said. "We'll go deal with this guy. But I'm not just handing this over." He passed the lead ball between his hands. I want something in return. That bastard killed my wife and two friends."

"We need to just put this behind us," Pete said. "He's got all the leverage. He's got the drugs and the hostages. What are we going to do?"

"I'll think of something. We call the Coast Guard, they're going to want to talk to us. The man here says he has the skills to deal with this, so let him," Jeff said.

They stopped the search and pointed the bow toward shore.

"You drive." Jeff handed the wheel to Trufante.

Trufante took the wheel and brought the boat up on a plane, spray flying as they cut through the waves. He tried to put Mac and the pain from his mind as he navigated toward the dock at Monster Bait. He had to get those girls to safety, or Mac would never forgive him. It meant leaving Mac out there for the time being — which he didn't like to do — but they'd be back for him soon. If they could find him.

As for Cesar, he wouldn't expect him to bring the boat in there. He could reach the dock a good half-hour before the meeting time. If there was a chance to surprise him and make a move, this was it. Cesar would be looking toward the road, not the docks.

* * *

Mac surfed each wave on his back, riding it until it fell into a trough, then finning to catch the next one. His training had taught him that this was the most efficient method for long swims with gear. He shivered as he looked over his shoulder at the lighthouse, it's white light blinked every ten seconds. The light on top of the 142-foot tower marking Sombrero reef was getting closer. Maybe a quarter mile he figured, using some quick geometry, that he'd been two miles away when he started. The base of the lighthouse had been invisible when he had began his swim. His body was starting to shut down from exhaustion and hypothermia. Fortunately the current was helping him towards his goal. He kept a steady pace for an hour. A white light suddenly appeared on the water. As the mast and then the sailboat came into view he pushed harder, reassured that he could get out of the water. Ten minutes later he was at the dive ladder, startling the couple on deck.

"Hey, can you help a guy out?" he yelled from the water.

It took a minute before a head appeared over the side of the ladder. It looked right at him and pulled back. He could hear voices, but not make out the conversation.

"We've got to help him," the man said.

"What if he's a pirate or smuggler or something?" Mac heard the woman. He was floating on the surface, his BC inflated, holding onto the dive ladder.

"We can't just let him sit out here. I'll call the Coast Guard and see what's up."

A few minutes later, both heads appeared over the side.

"Can you give a hand?" he gasped, nearly spent. He needed to get out of the water. After at least two hours, between the dive and the swim, even the eighty degree water could induce hypothermia.

They pulled him onto the boat, out of breath, exhausted from the effort.

"We were going to head into Boot Key and anchor there for the night. It's getting a little nautical out here,"the man said.

156

"We'll get you ashore before we anchor.

Mac took off the tank and BC then collapsed on the deck.

* * *

The buoy marking the entrance to Knights Key was close when he came to. He scanned his body checking for injury. The couple had given him a blanket and he had finally warmed up. Hypothermia was no longer a threat and he seemed fine, except for the joint pain and headache. Knowing the symptoms of decompression sickness was one thing; fixing it now was out of the question. He didn't have time to get to a hyperbaric chamber — he had to get to Mel and Jules. The woman appeared with a bottle of water. He rubbed the cold plastic against his head as he reviewed everything he could remember about the bends.

"You okay?" the woman asked.

"Yeah, thanks for everything. My place is just up about a half mile. Would you mind dropping me there?"

"Sure thing," the man answered. Mac could tell from his expression that he was relieved to get him off the boat -- still alive.

The ten minutes it took to reach his dock passed in silence, the boat moving at the five-mph harbor speed limit. His dock was dark and empty as the man helped offload the dive gear, and Mac said thank you and goodbye. As the boat pulled away, he left the gear on the dock and headed up to the house. He yanked at the crime scene tape, tearing it in half, and rolled up the garage door. With the exception of the blood, tape, and numbered markers on the floor, the workshop and his office looked as he had left them. Once in the office he grabbed the laptop and headed upstairs. In the bathroom he grabbed a handful of aspirin, went back to the kitchen and downed them with a shot of scotch. He eyed the bottle, taking two more hits from it as he waited for the computer to boot up.

The screen came to life, icons popping up one by one. He went to the internet browser and then to his wireless carrier, clicked on the option to track his phone, took another shot from the bottle, and waited for the spinning wheel on the screen. With his tendency to lose his phone, Mel had installed the software to help locate it. Finally a map displayed a red icon that represented his phone, the dot was moving through the harbor. He cursed himself for disconnecting his land line in favor of his cell phone, which meant he was now unable to call anyone. From the direction of the icon, it appeared that they were at Monster Bait.

He grabbed the truck keys, took the computer under his arm, and went after them.

Chapter 35

Cesar went to the bait shack alone, thankful for a couple of hours away from the terrorist. Ibrahim had taken the police SUV and gone back to Key West to pick up equipment to test the material. They'd been fooled once, and he had no intention of allowing that again. The story the Cajun had told about Mac being lost was not sitting well with him, either. In fact, this whole operation was upsetting his stomach. The yard was dark as he went to the bait shack, lit only by a few security lights. He debated whether to turn on the light in the bait shack or use the darkness as cover to surprise them. Then his military training kicked in. He turned on a single bulb and left the building, leaving the door slightly ajar and moving around the side to hide behind some traps. He checked his watch and waited. His quarry was coming to him, and when they got there he'd be ready.

* * *

Trufante nosed the boat to the dock, scraping the bow against the decaying boards. The old boards gave way instead of the fiberglass on the boat, and he and Jeff hopped onto the dock and tied off the boat.

"Dude, y'all ought to stay with the boat. Just in case we need to get out of here, ya know? He's expecting me, but doesn't know about the two of you. Probably ought to leave her running. There's no one here to hear the engine," Trufante said quietly as he looked around. He didn't want any interference from these two. His youth had been spent stalking creatures in the bayou. This would be no different.

"I'm going with you. Someone needs to protect our interests here," Jeff said.

He thought about the request and agreed. Two men would be better than one if it came to a fight. "Stay back, then. Y'all got any kind of weapons on this rig?" Trufante looked around the boat. "Hand me that gaff. The speargun wouldn't hurt, either."

Jeff took the speargun from Pete and pulled the bands back to load the weapon. Spearguns were efficient at close range in the water, but were even more deadly on land. Without the resistance of the water to temper the speed of the spear as it was released, it could penetrate bone at close range. The gaff was handed up to Trufante. It made for an awkward weapon, but was the best he had.

* * *

Cesar was watching the road when he heard the crunch of gravel. He glanced from behind the trap pile he was using as cover out into the yard, listening and watching, and heard it again, surprised that it came from the direction of the dock. A smile crossed his face ... they would never suspect this. If he had remained in the bait shack they could have taken him by surprise. He quietly moved to the other side of the stack which provided a better view. Two figures came into view, both holding what looked like sticks. Gun removed from his waistband, he leveled it and released the safety.

They approached the shack and paused before opening the door. He'd anticipated this, and took the opportunity to release from his stance, coming to stand behind them now, unnoticed.

"Put the stick down, Cajun. You too." He motioned to the men, as they dropped their weapons, to go inside. Gun drawn he followed, kicking their weapons to the side as he entered behind them. The taller man was looking at the chum machine and he grinned. "Bring back some memories, Cajun? Don't worry, my friend is not here. Where is the box?"

"You can slow your ass down there. You can have your box,

but we want the women first."

"Who are you to give me orders? You're sounding a little too brave, Cajun."

"You bastard." Jeff moved forward.

Cesar reacted immediately and shot at the floorboards. "Don't think you're important, *gringo*. Yes, I remember you. You are supposed to have some money for me as well."

Trufante had to hold Jeff back. He was becoming hysterical. "You killed her! You didn't even wait the twenty-four hours you gave me, you just killed both of them!"

"My deepest regrets about that. Sometimes things do not work out as one plans." He looked at Trufante. "Where is the box? I do not have the patience to ask again."

"I don't have it. It's on a boat circling out in the harbor, waiting for my signal," Trufante said. "The driver has the DEA on speed dial. I'm sure they would like to have a talk with you. Me, though, I believe in our relationship, and my friend here is looking for some restitution for his wife."

"Restitution? You idiot. You don't even know what it means." He pointed the gun at Trufante.

"It means we're not giving you the material without the release of the women and half the coke. That leaves you enough to break even on this whole deal and get the turban heads off your back. You get out with your skin. We get a little something for our trouble, and the girls go free."

Cesar watched the men, wondering how Trufante had all of a sudden grown some *huevos*. He decided to play it cool. Maybe there was something going on that he didn't know about. "Okay, Cajun. I see your point. How do you propose we make this exchange? I do not have the drugs with me."

"Easy, then. We meet at your house in Key West in two hours. That would be midnight. Have the girls there, and I'll leave the authorities out of it."

"How do I know I can trust you?" Cesar asked.

Trufante waved his bandaged finger at him. "Respect." With that, Trufante and Jeff walked out, picking up the speargun and gaff on the way.

* * *

"Well?" Pete asked, anxious to know what had happened.

"Hurry! Get out of here before he changes his mind," Trufante yelled. He went forward to untie the line.

Pete quickly put the boat in reverse, not waiting for Trufante's signal. He heard a scream as Trufante's finger caught in the knot as he backed. Seconds later the cleat tore from the rotting dock. He steered the boat towards the channel.

"Okay. We're clear. So what happened?" Pete asked.

"I'll tell you on the way. We go back to your place, grab a vehicle, and head to Key West. He's going to make the trade there."

"You really going to trust that piece of shit?" Jeff asked.

"Hell no, but down there we got a couple of things going for us. It's better to meet in a crowded neighborhood than this place," he waved his finger at the yard. Hopefully the drive will calm him down and he'll just make the exchange. "What about the coke?"

"Bonus if it works out, but let's focus on getting the women," Trufante said.

* * *

The twelve-seat propeller plane touched down at Key West International and taxied to a stop. The pilot cut the port engine and signaled for the flight attendant to drop the door. Mist sprayed from the AC vents as the conditioned air met the humid night. The passengers rose, jockeying for position to exit, all wanting to be the first to hit Duval Street and start their vacations.

Garcia waited in his seat for the aisle to clear, then rose and exited the craft, thanking the flight attendant and pilot on his way out the door. He followed the rest of the passengers into the terminal, then went straight for the exit. A black SUV pulled up, slowing slightly as he opened the door and hopped in.

"Thanks, man, owe you one," he said to the driver.

"Good to see you again," the driver answered.

"Were you able to bring the laptop?"

"You got it." He nodded over his shoulder at the briefcase in the backseat. "A FISA warrant opens all the doors. Who are we after?" the local FBI agent asked.

"Some guy name of Mac Travis. They're thinking he's tied up in some terrorist action with some Mexicans. Ask me, it looks like smuggling, but who am I to question?"

"You got that right, brother."

Garcia reached for the briefcase and opened it on his lap. The military-grade laptop inside whirled to life, and he started pecking out commands as the SUV left the airport and headed onto US1.

Chapter 36

Mel and Jules rummaged through the kitchen cabinets, assembling enough ingredients to make a meal while Jose sat at the bar, his gun resting on the counter. She was glad Cesar had left ... and the crazy factor with him. Jose seemed much calmer without his boss breathing down his neck.

"You know, you let us walk, I'll cut a deal for you. No jail. Maybe probation." Jules gave her best pitch.

Jose just nodded. He rarely talked, and she wondered if it was a language thing. *"Usted sabe, usted nos deja caminar, voy a hacer un trato para usted. No la cárcel. Tal vez la libertad condicional."* His look remained the same.

"No use. He understands. Actually pretty smart not to talk to us," Jules said.

Jose remained seated, drinking from a bottle of water.

This was their best chance to escape. The Middle Eastern man and Cesar had left. They couldn't overpower Jose, but there might be another way. Jules brushed up against her, trying to get her attention. "Keep him busy. I've got an idea."

Mel nodded, and Jules turned to Jose. *"El bano, por favor."*

Jose nodded to Jules, allowing permission. There were two bathrooms near the kitchen. She chose the powder room off the living room, hoping it would have a window visible from the street. Once inside, she turned on the light and checked the window. It slid up, revealing the handle on the hurricane shutter. She gently eased the shutter open, jumping as it creaked in its track. Escaping by herself was not really an option, as it might cost Mel her life, but this could be their way out. She looked for something to block the light under the door, but the towels were all small hand towels, the drapes translucent. It took her a long minute to realize that she was standing on a rug that would work. She moved aside, rolled it up, and pushed it against the door. It was more rigid than she had hoped, but she had no options.

Hoping Mel would buy her some time, she started flicking the light switch. The chances of anyone seeing her were minimal, but she had to try. *Dot - Dot - Dot - Dash - Dash - Dash - Dot - Dot - Dot.* She repeated the Morse code distress signal over and over, trying not to rush.

Then the butt of the gun struck the door, and she knew her time was up. "Just a second!" she called out. She turned off the light, set the rug back in place, then closed the shutter and window. One last look around to make sure the room looked the same, and she exhaled and opened the door.

Jose lowered the gun as she slithered her way around him, doing her best to look natural. He looked in the room and turned to her.

"Mujeres," was all he said.

* * *

The lobby of the sheriff's office was empty as well, the desk behind the plexiglass barrier vacant. Mac called out for help and started to pace the floor. He was about to yell out again when a woman appeared.

"Can I help you?" she asked through the speaker phone.

"Yeah. Name's Mac Travis. You're missing your sheriff and she's with my girlfriend."

The woman glanced at him, her face registering understanding, and he knew he had her. "Hold on, I'll buzz you through," she muttered.

Mac grabbed the handle and met resistance until the buzzer went off. He entered the working part of the station, which was as deserted as the front, and glanced around. "This place looks like a ghost town."

"They're all out looking for the sheriff. I'm Heather. I do the crime scene stuff here when they have something for me." She looked at Mac again. "Coffee?"

"That'd be great, but I need some help. Quickly. Can you find a deputy for me?" Mac said.

"I'm all you've got. Jules is my friend, though, and if she's in trouble I'll do anything to find her."

"Crime scene stuff? You know how to track cell phones?" he asked. His computer had stopped tracking as soon as the WiFi signal from his house was lost. With nowhere else to turn he had come here.

"I can do that. You need a court order for that, though."

"What if it's mine?"

"That's different. I need some information from the phone, though. If you don't have it, I can't set it up in the computer."

"I've got a program on my laptop that can find it. I've lost it enough to install the tracking software."

"How's finding your phone going to help us?"

Mac went back over the story as quickly as he could. He made an on-the-spot decision to trust this girl; the look on her face when she mentioned the sheriff being her friend had revealed enough.

"Where's the computer?"

"I've got it in the truck outside. I didn't think about it needing internet to work."

She looked skeptical. "You sure this is going to lead to them?"

"It's the only thing I," he paused, "*I* mean *we* have to go on."

"Okay, here's the deal. I help you do this, I'm with you the whole time. This is important to me personally, as well as professionally. You ditch me, I'm coming back here and calling every number for every local and federal agency that can make your life miserable. Understood?"

Mac just nodded as he walked out to get the computer.

Chapter 37

Trufante rode shotgun while Jeff drove and Pete leaned over the console from the backseat. He had a plan. But Jeff's need for revenge and Pete's waffling made him doubt their abilities. They were close to the Bahia Honda bridge, on their way south. The car had been quiet so far, but it was clear from Pete's body language that he had something to say.

"Dude, you're fidgeting like a teenage girl before the prom. Got something on your mind, spit it out." Trufante leaned back and eyed him.

"I just think we should have some kind of plan. Maybe we should call Homeland Security or the sheriff of something. You two seem more interested in getting the coke than making sure that stuff doesn't get in the wrong hands. I saw the guy he handed that box to. Definite terrorist."

"You're whining like a girl back there. We can do both," Jeff said. "We take the guy by surprise and get our coke back. Then we can call the Feds or whatever and leave the plutonium and the other dude for them."

"You two are giving me a headache," Trufante said, cranky now, the pain meds almost fully washed out of his system. "What about the women he's got for hostages? That's got to be the first priority. That dude leans a little to the crazy side, if you haven't noticed."

"We got to get the coke. Make him pay," Jeff said.

"Shut up, I got an idea coming." He shook his head to clear it, tendrils of hair flying around and almost catching Pete in the face. "Okay, here goes. The feds don't know nothing about the coke or the boom stuff. It's their deal to handle hostage situations. Maybe we call them in and let the SWAT team clear the house for us. Free the girls, take care of Cesar and anyone else around. Once they have what they want, we move in and find the coke."

"Damn, that works for me," Jeff said.

"Yeah, I'm okay with that too. What about the bomb stuff?" Pete said.

"I don't know, but with Cesar gone we can just hide it or something." Trufante was thinking big picture, details to follow.

"Deal, I'm in. What about you guys?" Jeff extended his fist for a three-way bump.

Before their fists hit, a truck loaded with propane tanks pulled off ahead of them. Jeff braked as he saw something rolling towards them. The cylinder was picking up speed, bouncing wildly down the road towards them. Jeff tried to swerve, but the tank caught on the dangling headlight, and the car skidded. Within moments, they heard the whoosh of the tank opening up. They had a gas leak directly under their car.

"Dude, pull over!" Trufante screamed at Jeff.

"I can't!" he returned, as he slowed to avoid another driver. Before he could get to the side, the shoulder disappeared as the road narrowed toward the bridge. Oncoming traffic made it impossible to pull onto the other side.

Instead, he braked. The car slowed, causing the tank's base to catch in the asphalt. It slid farther under the car. The wires from the broken headlight separated and sparked, the twelve volts enough to ignite the air escaping from the tank. The small flare turned to a loud explosion as the flame was sucked into the tank.

They looked backwards as the tank shot toward the propane truck, fire trailing it like a comet. The car shot forward, propelled by the blast.

"What do we do?" Pete asked.

"Forward," Trufante pointed without a second thought. "I need a goddamned beer."

* * *

Mac and Heather saw the fireball erupt from the top of the Seven Mile Bridge. It was still several miles away, and they were untouched by the explosion, but it still made them nervous. He wondered if he was too late, and Mel was in the conflagration.

"That's not good," Heather said from the passenger seat.

"No, I think we need a change in plans. Even if it didn't blow the bridge, they'll close the road for hours." He pounded the steering wheel, hoping he wasn't right. With the only road through the Keys closed he needed a backup plan.

"There's no other way through. What are we going to do now?" Heather asked.

"Boat. Only way around this mess."

Heather nodded and glanced at the computer screen. "The phone's still moving. They must be on the other side of it."

"Damn!" He knew Trufante had his phone. Figured he has something to do with this, he thought. Relieved that maybe Mel was still safe, Mac pulled off as soon as they hit Duck Key and turned around, facing back toward the bridge. First responders sped by, sirens blaring, and he waited impatiently, then floored the accelerator, the truck sprayed gravel behind it as they headed back toward Marathon.

Ten minutes later, they pulled into Mac's driveway. He jumped out of the car and went to the house. "Around back. I gotta grab a few things. I'll meet you on the boat."

Mac entered the house and grabbed two jackets and the other gun from the safe.

Chapter 38

Cesar was clearly agitated, snapping at Jose. He'd almost driven by the shuttered house when he saw the bathroom light blinking. He was looking for a dark, shuttered house. Realizing it was indeed the right house, he pulled over across the street and watched. How could Jose be so stupid? Several cars and a truck drove by as he watched. He pulled into the driveway as soon as the shutter was reinstalled and the room dark.

He opened the garage and pulled in, hitting the button to close the door before he was even out of the truck. "What the fuck was that?" He stormed into the house.

"What're you talking about?" Jose responded.

"The bathroom. Who was just in there?"

Jose pointed towards Jules. "What's the deal?"

"Oh nothing, you freaking moron." He stared down the women. "So, I drive by the house and a light is on. She could have escaped if she wanted. You're lucky she just tried to send a distress call." He moved toward Jules. "Don't think you're going to get away with that anymore. I'll watch you myself. Tie them up. Hands behind their backs."

Jose went to work on the restraints. He searched the drawers and pantry, coming back with a roll of duct tape.

"You don't need to tie us up. What you need to do is let us go. I'm sure there are half a dozen agencies trying to find us already!" Jules said.

"Put a gag in that one while you're at it. And the other one, too. I'm tired of listening to them," Cesar said.

They left the house, leaving the door unlocked. Cesar got in the driver's seat and watched as Jose pushed the girls into the backseat of the truck. He was impatient, but drove slowly now. It wouldn't be a good idea to get pulled over for a speeding ticket. The truck pulled out onto US1, heading south. He had to pull over twice before they hit the Seven Mile Bridge, for emergency vehicles. His heart rate increased every time he looked in the rearview mirror and saw the flashing lights coming up behind him. Finally, he realized they were not after him and relaxed. The last group had markings from Islamorada, forty-five minutes away. Whatever was going on, it had to be big.

The brake lights were visible as they hit the crest of the Seven Mile bridge. The lights stretched from the Bahia Honda Bridge back to Duck Key, and into the night. No headlights were coming in their direction, either — a sure sign that the road was closed.

"Crap. We need another plan. Look at this shit." He spun out into the empty oncoming traffic lane, executed a U-turn, hitting the curb on the other side rather than using a tamer three-point turn, and sped back toward Marathon.

"What you got in mind, boss?"

Cesar ignored him and drove back to the shuttered house. "Get them back in there. Watch everything. They don't pee without you staring in the bowl."

Alone now, he headed back north, an idea forming. He slowed as the airport came into sight on his left. Security lights illuminated the facility, housing mostly small planes. Another emergency vehicle blazed by as he waited to make a left turn into the service entrance. The access road led him to several hangers and he parked behind one, darker than the rest, its security lights out. Exiting the truck, he looked around for anyone watching and circled the building before entering through the open hangar doors. The building was empty. He went back toward where he assumed the bathrooms would be and found a changing room. Hanging on hooks by the door were several jump suits. He quickly put one on, then grabbed a screwdriver and wire cutters from the workbench on his way out to the tarmac.

His boots were the only thing that were incongruous with a mechanic, but he wasn't losing them. He'd risk it. Planes were parked side by side, chocks under their wheels, a chain securing each wing to a tie-down secured to the ground. He passed by several small jets, looking for a single-engine craft in which he would be comfortable.

The Cessna 172 with floats for water landings was just what he had in mind. Parked between two larger planes, it sat in the shadows, and he was able to do a quick visual inspection and remove the tie-downs. The lock popped through the thin sheet metal as soon as the butt of the gun hit the screwdriver. He climbed into the cockpit, searching for a flashlight. Most pilots carried a light in their flight bag, though sometimes a spare was left aboard.

The access panel removed, he cut the wires, bypassing the simple ignition switch. Power went on and the instruments lit up. A quick calculation assured him that the fuel shown on the gauges was twice what he needed to cross the forty-five miles to Key West. Once airborne, the flight would take less than thirty minutes.

He would have liked to do a complete preflight, the habit ingrained even in smugglers and outlaws, but the quicker he got the bird in the air the better. The magnetos spun and fired the single engine. It sputtered, turned over and caught. He allowed the gauges to settle and pulled into the taxi lane, running lights out, radio off. He would be able to see anyone approaching and have plenty of time to react.

Marathon, like most small airports, did not have an air traffic tower. The pilots relied on each other, calling in on standardized frequencies to alert other planes of their intentions. He scanned the sky as he pulled onto the runway and made sure the windsock was pointing towards him. No lights were on as he revved the engines and started his takeoff. The plane accelerated down the dark runway, only its shadow visible with its running lights off, and lifted into the air.

Several minutes later he had reached cruising altitude and gotten acclimated to the plane. It was clear from the air that he'd made the right choice. He turned the plane 180 degrees, heading west, and could see the fire and emergency vehicles struggling to secure the site on the bridge. Traffic was backed up in both directions for miles. The plane was cruising parallel to US1 now, navigation made easy as he followed the overseas highway toward Key West. His problem now was where to land. Key West International, another small airport, did not have a controller at night, but ICE was located there and he wanted nothing to do with customs or immigration. If he approached the airport, he would be picked up on radar. A sea landing off Stock Island was his best option to go in undetected.

He banked the plane toward the Gulf side and started his descent. Flying low to avoid other craft and radar, he could see the tops of each wave. Finger channels ran north and south, parallel in this area. He selected one and made a reconnaissance run, a quick low-altitude pass before landing, checking for obstructions in the water and small boats not visible from altitude. Then he turned and started his descent. He let his instincts take over, honed from the many times he'd done just this running drugs.

He slowed the plane and started to descend. Several minutes later, the floats hit water, causing the plane to bounce on a wave before settling into the trough. He backed the engines, slowing the speed further. The plane put out a wake sending several birds from their roosts in the adjacent mangroves. Gradually it slowed and once at a stop, he breathed for the first time in minutes. Now for ground transportation. He took Mel's phone from a pocket in his coveralls and turned it on. The blinking light on the maps app showed his position. A quick search of the cabin revealed an

inflatable raft and two oars, common safety gear in this area. He
popped the CO2 cartridge and tossed the inflatable into the dark
water. Once the CO2 cartridges had emptied and the raft inflated,
he pulled the raft toward him, placing it parallel with the pontoon.
Hoping his boots would not puncture the material he grabbed hold
of the raft and got in one careful foot at a time. He grabbed the oars
and settled into a rhythm, thanking his gods the tide was in his
favor.

* * *

Garcia sat in the parking lot, watching his laptop screen. The
FISA warrant allowed access to Mel and Mac's phones in real
time. How Davies had gotten them classified as potential terrorists
was beyond him, but not his concern. Mac's phone, displayed as a
green icon, had been moving erratically around Marathon for the
last hour. It was now over water, running under the Seven Mile
Bridge, showing a speed of thirty knots. The screen lit up with a
blue icon near Stock Island, indicating Mel's phone. This was the
first time he had seen her phone on. He zoomed in on the signal,
trying to project its course.

It looked like Travis was heading toward Key West,
probably coming by boat, he thought. Must have been stopped by
that bridge closure. The girl's phone looked like it was in the
water, moving slowly toward Stock Island.

Chapter 39

Red, white, and blue lights erupted from the top of the police car as it slowed slightly and executed a tight U-turn. Jeff's adrenaline shot a notch higher as he slowed, pulling off the main road onto the gravel shoulder. The officer was out of his car and moving toward them when Jeff opened the door.

"Freeze." The officer drew his gun and set his feet in a shooter's stance. "On the ground, now."

"I was only--"

"I don't care. On the ground. You two, out of the car, hands first. Lock them behind your head and get on your knees." The cop leaned his head toward his lapel and spoke into the mike.

Trufante and Pete complied, the gravel digging into their knees as they waited. Jeff was flat, spread eagle, on the ground. The officer approached and frisked him. Finding no weapons, he ratcheted the cuffs on Jeff's wrists and applied pressure with his billy club. Jeff winced in pain as he was forced to his feet, his shoulders feeling like they were about to pop out of their socket.

"Y'all been drinking?"

"No, sir, been wanting one for a while though," Trufante said revealing his teeth with a wide grin.

"Your headlight is out and your muffler's dragging. Y'all could start a fire like that." He walked around the car, inspecting it as he went. "That looks like a burn mark on the passenger side where the tail pipe was dragging. Where're y'all coming from?"

Trufante started to answer, but caught a sharp look from the officer. Jeff stared him down, wishing him silent.

The cop shook his head and approached Jeff. "Well? I'll need to see some ID — license, registration, insurance."

Jeff held up his cuffed hands with a shrug. "License is in my back pocket. Registration and insurance are in the glove box. We were coming down from Big Pine. Looking for a little party action."

The officer pulled Jeff's wallet from his pocket and extracted the license. He went to the glove compartment and started sorting through the stack of paper. Registration and insurance in hand, he told the men to wait where they were and went back to his car.

Their knees were numb from kneeling when he came back.

"Seems like I need to take you in. I'm thinking you started that fire on Bahia Honda. That got a ring of truth to it?" "It was an accident," Pete said. "We weren't even sure it was us until we saw the tail pipe just now. Felt like something hit the car."

"Whatever. In the car — backseat, all three of you. I have orders to take you in."

"We didn't do anything," Jeff said.

"You 'bout blew that bridge off its pilings. Accident or not, we'll figure that out at the station. There's all kinds of Feds waiting to talk to someone. Might as well be you."

He shined his flashlight in the back windows after the men were locked in the back of his car. The backpack with the lead ball was sitting on the seat. He reached in and grabbed it.

* * *

The station was bustling with activity when the officer escorted the three men through the door and started the booking process. Garcia lounged by the coffee machine, soaking it all in. He'd heard about the explosion in Bahia Honda when he landed and, not believing in coincidences, had driven directly to the police station to check it out. There were agents in every corner, talking to their bosses on cell phones. The media were amassing at the entrance, testing their theories on each other, hoping theirs would be the one that would stick. Two hours after the explosion it was the lead story on every cable channel. He sat back, just watching the incompetent wheels of government bureaucracy spin. The phone vibrated in his pocket. The agent that picked him up had followed through and sent him the pictures he'd asked for. He scanned through them, committing to memory any identifying marks. He laughed out loud when he saw Trufante's picture. The smile left his face when he looked up and saw the same man being escorted in.

He approached the booking desk, eavesdropping on the conversation as he got closer. Before the officer could lead them to be fingerprinted, he presented his ID to the officer.

"Mind if I have a word with this one?" He pointed to Trufante. "Homeland has him red flagged."

"No problem. I can set you up in a room over here." He led the party down the hall, opened the door, and let Garcia and Trufante in. "I'll be back for him. Let me process these two and I'll come back. Just don't leave him alone until I return."

Garcia signaled Trufante to the far chair and pulled out his own chair, across the table from him.

"You want to tell me what's going on here?" he asked. This was his usual opening line when he didn't know anything. Let them spill whatever they would. Quiet was often the best interrogation tool. He'd put the pieces together as it went.

"Crap, man, I could use a beer and a pain pill. Goddamned finger's throbbing like a gut hooked fish."

"Sorry, bud, can't help you there. Why don't you help me out? Tell me your story and I'll get you a Coke or something."

"I got a story'll get me a shot of rum in that Coke."

Trufante held the stump up for Dougherty to examine. "This son of a bitch chopped off the tip of my finger in a bait grinder."

"You're a big help. What about the explosion at Bahia Honda?" Garcia looked down at the printout in front of him. "This

177

is a pretty thick file for someones who's never been in real trouble. Seems you just wind up in the wrong place at the wrong time." He thumbed through the printouts.

"Amen, brother. Yeah, about the blowup ... we were just passing through--"

Garcia cut him off, "Maybe you give me something to work with, I'll get you a doctor. I'm sure he'll give you something for that."

"Hell, yeah. Deal man."

Garcia stared at the stump as Trufante was finishing his story. "So, that's it? You guys found a bunch of coke and instead of turning it in, or just leaving it floating out there, you had to go try and get rich off it?"

"Something like that, but I didn't find it or decide to keep it. I just helped those dudes broker it. You know, trying to help them out. There's something else you ought to know about." He relayed the story of the box.

Garcia starred at him.

"What about the doc?"

"I'll see what I can do about that."

As Garcia was leaving Trufante called out, "They brought a backpack in with us. We're going to need that."

* * *

Cesar walked the last half mile from the harbor to his house as dawn was breaking. He stripped off the jumpsuit, wet with sweat. The temperature was a balmy eighty degrees, humidity in the 90's. He reached in his pocket for the house key. Realizing it had been left on the plane, he jimmied the back door with the screwdriver in his pocket. Once inside he headed upstairs for a quick shower.

Turned all the way to cold, which was actually tepid in the subtropical environment, water washed the grime off but did nothing for the fatigue. The last few days had left a trail of dead bodies and lost opportunity. He dismissed these, though, and focused on the gold pieces he'd taken from the *gringo's* safe. He looked at the pattern intricately tattooed on his arms. The symbol came up at least a dozen times, a sea serpent snaking through the elaborate patterns. The tattoos were a deliberate pattern, not unlike the simpler gang ink, but more complex. The members of his cartel could all trace their lineages directly from Chontal Mayan ancestors. This was the first requirement of the cartel — a blood line unblemished by the Spaniards. This earned the first in a series of tattoos. The rest had to be earned as he'd climbed from poverty to the top tier. It was said that the patterns held secrets that would be revealed to the wearer in time, but he had yet to be enlightened.

He finished in the shower, dried off, and dressed. In the kitchen he opened a Coke and picked up his phone. Diego answered on the first ring, eager for an update. Once Cesar assured him the call was being made from a burner phone, the details of the last few days were revealed.

"So, you are waiting to make the exchange?"

"*Si, jefe*. Should be any time now. I have a concern, though, about where the sand heads are going to set the bomb off. Even if they took it to Miami, that would be bad for business."

"Listen to me, Cesar. Those guys couldn't light a cigarette with a blow torch. The chances of them doing any kind of damage are minimal. Key West is pretty much played out as an import point. Let them blow that piece of coral to their heaven. I am thinking of Louisiana. We find someone that knows that bayou country, no one will catch us. That is our concern. Let the US government put all their assets around the Keys. We'll be long gone."

"Brilliant, as usual. I knew you had thought this through. It happens I have just the man to show us the ropes in Louisiana."

"Excellent, Cesar. Finish this transaction."

Chapter 40

Heather came out of the cabin, shaking her hair, and rubbing the sleep out of her eyes.

"How long have I been out?"

"Couple of hours. I cut the speed down to fifteen knots to save fuel. Running any faster, we would have run out."

"You want me to take the wheel for a while so you can get some rest? You look like you need it."

"No, I'm good. We're almost there anyway." He looked down at the chart plotter, which showed their position as they moved through the channels leading to Key West. He rubbed his neck muscles. "Why don't you get that computer of yours set up and see where my phone is."

She went below and emerged a few minutes later. "I can't get a signal on it. We need to get closer."

"Fifteen, twenty minutes we'll be in the harbor. I'm sure we can hijack a Wi-Fi signal from one of the resorts there."

They sat back in silence, watching the mangroves lining the channels slide by. Soon the tops of sailboat masts were visible. It took another five minutes running at idle in the protected harbor before Heather yelled up that she had a signal.

She brought the laptop to the console to show him. "It's here on the island. Give me a minute and I'll transpose the coordinates onto a map." He watched from the corner of his eye as she manipulated screens. "You're not going to believe this. It's at the police station."

"Led by the King of the Idiots, how else was this going to go?"

"It's not all bad. They call me down there from time to time. I can walk in there and probably get it back for you."

"Thanks, but that doesn't help. We need them to take it to the exchange so we can follow."

"Let me go in and see what's going on, anyway. It wouldn't hurt to have some more information."

"As long as you keep this between us. All I want is to get the girls back."

"Yeah, me too. I'm with you."

"There's a dock over there. Bound to be a bicycle that's unlocked. Can you find the station from there?"

"Like a rooster can find a hen house. Probably take me an hour to get there, see what's going on and get back here."

"Take the number off this burner phone. Call me when you're ten minutes out and I'll come get you."

* * *

Patel stood on the balcony of Ibrahim's house, his clothes clinging to his body as he dialed the phone. He would have preferred the AC of the room, but was always cautious about bugs and chose the humidity instead. Davies was not picking up though and he was getting impatient. Ibrahim was waiting downstairs.

He put the phone in his pocket and went back inside, wondering where Davies was. He needed confirmation the president would be here. Ibrahim was in the kitchen when he entered, "Have you heard from the drug dealer?"

"Not yet." Ibrahim sat at the table staring at the cell phone, willing it to ring.

"Go there. I don't trust him."

Ibrahim got up slowly, clearly in pain. He turned away from Patel, reached in his pocket for the bottle and took three pills. Before he left, he stopped at a desk and unclipped a gun from a hidden holster. "I'll keep you updated."

The phone rang as Ibrahim was on his way out the door and

Patel looked down at the screen for the caller ID. But the burner phone was an old-style flip phone. He picked it up and flipped it open. "Yes?"

"Garcia called. Seems Travis is missing, maybe dead. He's at the Key West police station. He told me there is a BOLO out for him." He paused, "There's something else going on, though. It seems that a cohort of his has his cell phone. He's being held at the police station in Key West," Davies said.

"That is all you have?"

"What else do you want from me? I set up the meeting. I had my man track Travis," Davies said.

"I want you to call your man and find out what he knows about this man they have in custody. He could have something important." Patel didn't like all the moving parts going on here.

"What is this about? So I took some diamonds from a friend of yours as a payment for a very discreet favor, years ago. That doesn't mean I do everything you say. There's something wrong here, and I intend to find out what it is."

"I would recommend you think carefully about how you proceed. It may have been a long time ago, but I don't think your associates will be as forgiving as you think."

Several seconds of silence followed. "All right. I'll find out what you want. Then we're done."

"As long as the president shows up for his speech, I will release you."

* * *

Davies hung up and took a deep breath. The doctors had told him to avoid stress, alcohol, and everything else life had to offer. Well, he had the stress, screw it, throw in some alcohol too. He went to the decanter and poured an inch into the tumbler. He paused and added another.

Then he dialed again. "Can you go someplace we can talk?"

"Go ahead," Garcia answered a minute later.

Davies paused, trying to figure out what Patel's angle in this was. "Is there one that could be the leader?"

"There's this Cajun guy, named Alan Trufante. He's in an interview room now."

"Can you get him released and keep an eye on him? I've got it on good authority that there's something bigger than the coke deal going on here."

"I'm not sure I can do that. I don't have jurisdiction here." He thought for a minute. "There is a way that might work. I can name him as a confidential informant who will only talk to me. I can probably just walk him out of here. There's so much confusion about the explosion that they won't really check. The thing is, I can't let him just go loose. If you want to find out what's going on I can put a wire on him. Let him go do whatever deal he has planned."

"That'll work." Davies drank half the tumbler. He sat back down and pulled a legal pad from his drawer. It took a while, but he laid out the entire history of what had happened since he had met Patel. He listed all the favors he'd been asked to do over the years, and placed them in a timeline. He went to his computer and pulled up a chronological sequence of terrorist activity since 1992, when he'd taken the diamonds. He was angered, but not surprised to see the connection.

Chapter 41

Heather keyed the code in the pad by the back door of the police station. The lock buzzed, allowing her to turn the knob. The scene unfolded as she slid through the room, looking for someone she knew who wasn't already occupied. Every seat was taken, every phone in use, and those not on a land line had their cell phones to their ears. She glanced in each interrogation room as she walked down the hall toward the restroom. Trufante caught her eye as she passed the room he was waiting in. Forgetting the bathroom, she entered the room.

"What are you doing here?" she asked.

"Seems trouble has a way of finding me." He leaned back in the chair.

"We already established that phenomena." She sat in the chair across the table. "What did you do now?"

Before he could answer, a man entered the room, papers and a pen in hand. He looked at Heather, then shifted his attention to Trufante and placed the papers in front of him. "Sign where it says. I got a doctor to see you, and we can get on with this."

"Get on with what?" Heather asked.

"And you are?" the man asked. "I'm Garcia, FBI."

She looked at Trufante. "Don't sign that." Then she turned to Garcia. "I'm with the CSI here. I know this man. He's a witness in a murder in Marathon. I need to take him back there," she bluffed.

"Are you charging him?" Garcia asked.

She paused, "No. But the sheriff--"

He cut her off. "The sheriff nothing. He has agreed to be a confidential informant with us. Your sheriff has a problem with that have him call me."

"Her. She's not going to like this."

He waved her off.

She stepped to the back wall of the room and watched as he explained the paperwork to Trufante. He seemed oblivious.

Trufante finished his signature and handed the papers to Garcia. "Sorry, girl. He promised to get me some pain pills."

She took a step toward the table figuring she might as well get as much information as she could. "What are you doing with him?"

"He's a CI." Garcia gave her a quick overview of the situation. "I'm gonna wire him up and let him make his deal. You said you're CSI, maybe you can help me."

"So, now you want my help. What's in it for me?"

"You can keep an eye on your friend here."

"I'll help you as long as you keep me in the loop." She needed to keep whatever little leverage she had.

"Okay, so we need to wire him up. You have access to the equipment here - let's see what you can put together. I need to hear and record everything from a hundred yards," Garcia said.

Heather left the room. She went toward the equipment room where the gear was stored, and selected what she needed. Thinking about Mac, she moved to the back of the storage area and pulled out her cell phone. Not sure if the burner phone could text, she called him, watching the door so as not to be overheard.

"You ready?"

"No, something's come up. They've got Trufante here, and I just cut a deal with an FBI agent to wire him up and follow."

"Can you let me know where you're going?"

"Can I text you on that thing?"

"I think so."

"I'll send you the address as soon as we set up. That's the best I can do."

"That'll work fine," he said.

She disconnected and went back to the interrogation room.

Trufante squirmed as she applied the tape that held the mike and wires to his body. "Drop your pants."

"Thought you didn't swing that way."

She shot him a look and waited. "Here, tape this to yourself. Right below your unit, inside your leg. Even a girl wouldn't frisk you there."

"You'd be surprised."

"Pull that earring out." She handed him another.

"What you got here?" Garcia asked.

"Camera. It doesn't have much for range, but it can't hurt. He'll never suspect it."

She turned to Garcia and nodded. "Ready."

They left the interview room and went single file toward the entrance. Garcia had the papers in hand, ready to present them to anyone questioning what he was doing removing a prisoner from custody. Heather caught a couple of looks on the way out and nodded back, but no one questioned them.

"Where's the meet?" Garcia asked Trufante as they found his rental car.

"Don't know the address, but I can get us there. What about that doctor?"

"Just get through this and I'll set you up. I can't have you going in there under the influence."

"Damn, man, I work better under the influence."

* * *

Cesar paced the ground floor of the house like a caged animal. He was wearing a groove in the old pine floor, going from window to window. He checked his watch again, then went to the kitchen to check on the girls. Jose had arrived at dawn with them.

They were late for the exchange, and Trufante's number went straight to voicemail. Again. As vigilant as he had been, the knock on the door startled him. He went to the wall and slid toward the closest window. His paranoia settled, although his anger red lined as he opened the door for Ibrahim.

"Use the back door. I don't need anyone seeing you come in here."

"Where are they?"

"Fuck if I know. They should have been here an hour ago."

"This had better happen, or the repercussions will be severe."

Cesar glared at him. The only good outcome in his mind was to put a bullet in the terrorist's head. Maybe he'd shoot him in the ear, see if sand came out the other end. Despite Diego's call, he moved toward the chair where his gun was hidden. He stopped short as he saw Trufante start up the walk outside.

"Go hide. He's here," Cesar called out to Ibrahim, who took off into the kitchen. Trufante lost his balance as he knocked on air, Cesar having already opened the door. "Get your Cajun ass in here. I've been waiting, and that's not good for your health. You got the stuff?"

Trufante slid the backpack off his shoulder.

"Not there, you idiot. In the house, away from the windows."

Trufante went to the stairs giving Cesar a questioning look. "Where are the girls? I'm not giving this over until I know they're safe."

Cesar went toward the kitchen and opened the door. "Tell him you're okay."

Trufante relaxed as he heard both girls' voices. He reached into the pack for a lead ball. "Here. Now, let them go."

"Not so fast, Cajun. You set me up last time. You think I'll allow that to happen again?" Cesar called out to the kitchen, and Ibrahim emerged through the door. He handed him the backpack and watched as he left the house hoping this would end their relationship.

"What now?" Trufante asked. "You got something for this?"

He held up his finger. "Son of a bitch hurts!"

Cesar ignored the request. "Now we wait for him to call and assure me that there has been no switch. Why don't you sit down? I have a proposition for you. Maybe a good opportunity."

Trufante sat on the stair. "You need me for something, I need something from you." He held up his bandaged stump. "This son of a bitch is throbbing like a gator in a net."

* * *

They sat in the SUV. The motor was running allowing the AC to keep the heat at bay. Heather fiddled with the controls. She was happy with the performance of the gear; they were able to see and hear everything going on inside the house.

"One's leaving. We have to split up. I'm going after him," Garcia said as he opened the door. "Keep an eye on our boy here."

"How do I reach you?" Heather asked.

Garcia pulled a card from his pocket and tossed it on the seat before he slammed the door and took off. Heather sat there, alone. She was relieved that Jules was safe, having clearly heard Jules and Mel respond on the surveillance equipment, but unsure how to proceed. Then her cell phone buzzed on her lap, bringing her back to reality.

"What happened?" Mac asked.

"Crap, I got so wrapped up in this I forgot to call you. Give me ten minutes. I'll pick you up in a black SUV at the dock where you dropped me off."

Chapter 42

Garcia followed the pink scooter through the busy streets. He didn't regret his decision to pursue on foot. With the nightly party in full swing, the traffic would have made it impossible for the SUV to follow the more agile scooter through the tight streets and crowds. The scooter was going the same speed as his fast walk, having to wait for pedestrians at every intersection. He sighed in relief as the driver passed perpendicular through Duval Street. The man would have been impossible to locate among the throng of partiers had he chosen to turn.

Garcia broke into a jog now that the scooter was out of traffic. Fortunately, the guy had pulled into a driveway, and he slowed to a walk, casually strolling by the house. There was nothing out of the ordinary to be observed from the outside, so he kept walking.

With two targets, he had to make a decision, but after hearing the girls voices, he knew he had to stay with the terrorist.

He was two houses past the target when he pulled out his phone. "Are you moving?" He heard road noise in the background of Heather's phone. "I thought I told you to stay put."

"There's someone else I need to bring into this. I'm picking him up now. Should I go back to the house?"

"You need to get back there now! I need you there." He paused, trying not to show his anger over the phone, "Do you still have the connection to the wire and camera?"

He waited for her to respond "No, I lost it."

"Hurry. Get whoever you're getting and get back in range

there. We need eyes on that house in case I'm chasing a red herring."

* * *

Heather drove like a maniac through the crowded streets. She knew leaving the house was wrong, but she needed Mac's help. Before the SUV came to a stop, Mac opened the door and hopped in on the run.

"Nice ride. Looks like the Feds."

"Yeah, but this guy seems like he's working on his own. He's pretty cool for one of them." Heather ran through the events of the past hour as she drove back to Cesar's house, where they'd left Trufante.

She parked a block away and rebooted the equipment. The camera showed a floor, moving back and forth, cowboy boots now in the picture.

"I know those boots."

"Sshh. They're talking."

Cesar was grilling Trufante about his knowledge of southern Louisiana. The Cajun was trying to explain the intricacies of the bayous and canals, and how the best route to bring in contraband was into a town called Venice, the first town up the Mississippi.

"Wonder what that's all about? Maybe thinking of blowing this popsicle stand and setting up shop there."

"I wish he'd move around a little and show the room. I'm dying to know if Jules is okay."

"Yeah, Mel too." He craned his neck to get a better view of the screen.

Heather's phone rang. "Yeah, I'm back on site. I have audio and visual." She put the phone on speaker.

"I'm thinking of calling a SWAT team into that house and letting them handle it. It's a pretty straightforward hostage situation, and that's what they train for. They'll think it's some kind of drug deal gone wrong."

"If you think that's the best way," Heather said.

"Listen, whoever you are, name's Mac Travis." He said loudly to the speaker, "I know exactly what's going on in there, and the people involved. I can get them out without SWAT."

"Mr. Travis, you are not an officer of the law, or authorized in any way to go into that house. Sit tight and wait for SWAT."

"We're not waiting for the SWAT team. No way, not with that unstable bastard in there. They look at him wrong and he'll shoot them. No. I'll get 'em out." Mac paused. "We have total surprise and Jules is trained for this. SWAT goes in there you're going to ruin two careers — Mel and Jules will never be able to explain how they went rogue and ended up captives to a drug dealer."

"Heather, are you still there?"

"Yeah."

"Under no circumstances is he to go after them, do you understand? I'm only allowing you to stay so we can maintain surveillance."

She hung up and stared at the monitor. The audio crackled. "Dude, they're going to blow us up."

"Cajun, what kind of *mierda* you talking?"

"You ain't going to be smuggling nothing through the bayou if you're dead. What if they blow that thing here?"

The camera showed the sidewalk outside the house now. "Mac, look." She shifted the laptop toward the passenger seat. "They're moving."

Mac was already looking at the street. "You don't need that thing. It's just the two of them — Cesar and Trufante. Where are the girls?"

* * *

Ibrahim fidgeted outside the closet-turned-safe-room badly needing more pain relievers, but he knew this was more important. Paradise was close and there would be no pain there. Patel had been inside for ten minutes now — plenty of time to confirm the contents of the lead ball. Finally the door opened and he emerged, stripping the protective gear off as soon as the door closed. He nodded.

"It's good?"

"Yes, Allah has blessed us. It is the correct material, just a little light. That can be attributed to the handling and residue left in the original box. You can call the drug dealer and tell him that we are through with him."

"No. Let him worry. It will keep him out of our hair. He's caused enough trouble already."

"Very good. I will leave that decision to you. It is time to assemble the bomb. Do you have the rest of the materials?"

"Everything but the primer. I was planning on forcing an explosion where the bomb will be placed. That will detonate the material."

"I would have preferred a self-contained unit."

"The bomb casing and shrapnel were easily obtained. The primer ingredients would have set off red flags. I think this is best."

"You are not the one to think here. Bring the material up here. I will pray and then start to assemble the bomb."

* * *

Davies walked off the stairs leading from Air Force One, breathing in the tropical night air. Black SUVs surrounded the plane as the passengers disembarked. The president was last and quickly whisked into an armored vehicle, identical to the others. The crowd started to disperse as the vehicle pulled away, the excitement over. The rest of the passengers — aides and press — warranted no attention. Davies walked toward the terminal, with only his carry-on and briefcase he went right to the street and into a waiting cab.

"Hyatt, please."

"Sure thing, man." The driver pulled out of the taxi line, heading for the airport entrance.

Half an hour later Davies checked into his room, ordered

room service and sat on the couch, pondering his next move. He was convinced something bad was going to happen here, he just didn't know what. Patel was either a terrorist or connected to a network. Thinking about it, the way he had blended into the top echelon of DC society so easily, portraying himself as Italian, he must be more than a low-level operative. He was likely very high up, if not a top leader.

With that thought, Davies dialed Garcia's number. "We need to talk."

"I'm a little busy right now. This thing with Travis has turned into more than we bargained for. Looks like he's one of the good guys. There's some kind of terrorist connection here with the drug cartel and some guys I'm staked out on now."

"You know what's going on here tomorrow?"

"Here? Are you in town?"

"Yes, but so is the president. He's scheduled to give a speech on gay rights tomorrow morning. Here."

"Shit, we've got a problem. I've got to call in some higher ups. This is way over my pay grade."

"Let's walk this through before you call. It's almost ten now. The speech is at nine tomorrow. That's less than twelve hours. It'll take the big wigs that long just to assign units. On top of that, they're all over that explosion up at the Bahia Honda Bridge. What assets are you in control of?" Davie's practiced tone portrayed enough authority to redirect Garcia's attention.

"I'm working with a CSI from Marathon. Travis is with her. They're watching a drug dealer who has hostages, one of whom is the sheriff from Marathon. I'm following guys who look like they might be trouble. Middle Eastern. That's all I've got."

"Okay, I'm going to direct this from here. I'm at the Hyatt. You stay on surveillance. As long as we know where they are, we can contain this. I'll call for help when we need it."

Chapter 43

Mac watched the two men walk down the street.

"What do we do?" Heather asked.

"We can't split up. Let's get Jules and Mel, first. They're on foot. They won't get far, especially if there are four of us looking instead of just the two."

Mac got out of the car and started jogging toward the house, Heather right behind him. When they got close enough, Heather went to the living room window and peered in, while Mac tried the door. No one was visible, and the door was locked. They made their way around the house, checking all the other windows and doors. The kitchen had a small back deck, large enough for a barbecue grill, flower pots, and a table and chairs. Heather went to the window and stared intently into the room. Mac checked the side of the house.

"Mac, they're here! Come around!" she hissed.

He ran around to the deck and looked in the window. The girls were gagged and tied back to back. He saw Mel in distress and moved quickly to the door. The lock wouldn't budge. The solid wood door was old but looked sound. He stepped back, aiming for the doorknob with a front kick. His foot went entirely through the door, caving in the lock and releasing the latch. Pain engulfed him when he tried to remove his foot and the ragged splinters pierced his flesh.

He looked at Heather who was frozen in indecision. "I'll be okay. Get the girls." He hopped back on his good foot allowing the door to open. Once she was in, he reached forward and smashed in the wood around the splinters. His foot came free, several mean looking pieces of wood embedded in it. His injured leg throbbed and would not take weight as he hobbled in behind her and collapsed in the doorway.

She searched the kitchen drawers until she found a knife. Going to work on Jules first, she cut her free. Jules reached to her mouth and pulled off the duct tape. "Mac, are you alright?"

"Yeah," he replied, trying to pull the splinters free. They were so jagged it was like trying to remove a barbed fish hook and the old wood just dug deeper when he tried to remove them, enlarging the trauma. "Hurry up, we need to go after them."

"I've got surveillance on them." Heather went to Jules and hugged her.

Heather had Mel free now and the group stood over Mac. Mel went down to her knees to help him, "Mac, I--" she started to apologize.

"Never mind. You two have to go after Trufante and the drug dealer. Idiot's likely to get himself killed."

"What about you?" Mel asked.

He ignored her and spoke to Jules. "You guys go on foot. We'll follow in the SUV. See if Heather here can work the equipment and get a reading on them." He looked down at his blood soaked leg, "Don't think I'll be doing any running today."

"Which direction were they heading?" Jules asked. "Who's got a phone?"

Heather answered, "Toward Duval Street. Mac has the burner and I have mine."

"Good. Give me yours." Jules reached for the phone and they headed out the door.

Mac used the door jamb to gain his feet. He tried to walk on the injured foot and almost collapsed. Bright lights flashed in his head the pain was so bad. "You got any training?"

"Some. Stay here. I'll see if I can find any supplies."

Mac eased himself back to the floor to wait. He worked

several of the splinters free, but two large ones were deep.

"Let me see that," she said as she set an armful of supplies on the floor next to him. She went right to work on him, first cleaning the blood. As soon as she started prodding around the remaining splinters, he screamed in pain. "There's infection showing already. I couldn't find much but this." She held up a large baggie half full with white powder.

"What the hell are you going to do with that?"

"It's all we've got and I think it'll work." She reached into the bag and grabbed a handful despite his protests.

He watched as she started to rub the powder around the wounds. They quickly became numb.

"Okay, here we go." She grabbed one of the splinters and started working it around.

There was pain, but it was bearable now. He waited as she patiently worked the second splinter free. "Nice work. Patch it up and let's go."

She applied a generous dose of the cocaine to the open wounds and wrapped the entire lower leg with strips torn from a shirt she had found upstairs.

Chapter 44

Garcia watched the terrorist's house, wondering what was happening at the other site. He thought of calling again, but stopped himself as the door opened. The man he'd followed walked out and went toward the detached garage. The light came on. Garcia thought about changing position when the man's shadow became visible, moving back to the door. He was moving something awkward, but Garcia couldn't make out what it was until the guy wrestled it through the doorway. The 55-gallon drum rolled easily on its rim now that he was in the open. He reached the stairs to the house and stopped, looking for the best way to get the barrel up the flight of stairs. Two steps later, he looked up at the remaining stairs and reversed course. He left the barrel on the walk and went back into the house.

Garcia felt naked as he ran across the lawn to look at the barrel. He had to get a quick look, even if it exposed him. He could always continue down the street, trying to look like a jogger. He slowed when he reached the drum. It had appeared empty from the way the man had handled it, but he tapped it to be sure. There were no hazardous placards on it — just a plain blue barrel. He continued to the house next door and hid behind a bush.

Two men appeared at the door now. One was the man he'd been following, the other remained back in the house. Garcia wished he had some binoculars. The man in the shadows looked familiar, but he couldn't get a good enough look from where he was. They stared at the barrel speaking in hushed tones he could not understand. Both men turned at the same time and went back in the house.

* * *

Ibrahim looked at Patel. "It's too big to get upstairs."

"We have to assemble the bomb in the safe room. You should have thought about this before hand."

"I got everything on the list I was given."

"It's too late now. Put the barrel back in the garage. I will assemble as much as I can upstairs. Then we will have to finish it in the garage. You have transportation when we are done?"

"Yes, I have a truck available at seven a.m."

* * *

Trufante was dragging, despite Cesar's constant jabs. "We gotta move." The streets were insane, both with pedestrians and vehicles. It was like spring break every weekend here; traffic jammed at every corner and no parking for blocks. People, most carrying drinks wove in and out of traffic.

"What's your rush? Look at this. You're too stressed, man, you need to enjoy yourself more."

"We got business, you idiot. That's how you got in all this trouble — mixing business with pleasure."

Trufante ignored him and kept looking. He was walking backwards, his gaze following a group of coeds now, when he spotted Mel a half block behind. He quickly turned, hoping Cesar wouldn't notice. He knew Cesar was armed and unstable. Not sure if the crowds were enough of a deterrent to stop him from doing something rash, he chose to be conservative.

Somehow he had to make the craziness surrounding them work to his advantage. He glanced up and down the street and saw a busy bar. People moved steadily in and out of the crowded bar, the biggest and usually the loudest on the strip. Three bouncers were at the door checking IDs and making sure the crowd remained at the edge of madness, but not over it. It was a fine line to run a bar known for wild action.

Trufante made his move and crossed the street, heading for

the door. "I need a *bano*, man."

Cesar pulled his shirt from behind. "You go where I say."

"Dude, nature's calling. Chill."

Cesar didn't have any options. Unless he was going to shoot him in the street, he had to play along. "Hurry up. I'm not letting you out of my sight."

* * *

Jules spotted them crossing the street. "There they are. Mel, you see 'em?"

Mel saw Trufante lean over and shake the hand of one of the bouncers, clapping him on the back like an old friend, then disappear into the bar with Cesar right on his trail. Jules ran across the street, phone in hand, dodging cars as she followed close behind them. As they got to the door, the bouncer reached his arm out.

"ID."

Jules looked at him, then thrust her badge. "Here's your ID! Call 911, tell them you have an armed and dangerous man in there. That tall guy that just talked to you, he's cool. The other guy's the one we want. Send one of these clowns to the back door."

One of the bouncers took off around the corner, and Jules entered the bar, Mel following closely. The music had been loud outside, but it was a level higher in here. The band was playing a Jimmy Buffet cover, the dance floor packed. They had to walk sideways to move through the crowd, the thinner profile making it easier to squeeze through. The problem was, at five foot four and five foot five, they couldn't see anything.

"On the bar, girl. Point them out!" Jules yelled in her ear, pointing to the girls dancing on the bar.

"Been a long time," Mel said as she pushed through the crowd. She reached a group of guys huddled together doing shots, and yelled that she wanted a boost up. They happily complied, hoisting her onto the bar top. She remembered a line from Hunter

S Thompson: *When the going gets weird, the weird turn pro.* This was the scene around her. A couple of shots and maybe she could blend in, but sober, this was hard.

No one seemed to notice that she wasn't shaking like the other girls. She wiggled enough to move down the bar and spotted Trufante towering over the other revelers, heading toward the bathroom. She caught Jules's eye and pointed, then looked for an escape route, but it was futile. Help getting onto the bar was easy, not so much getting off. As Jules headed toward the bathroom, Mel watched stuck on the bar, oblivious to the music.

* * *

Mac was getting impatient. The pain had eased considerably and he was able to put some weight on his leg. Jules had called Garcia with an update as soon as they had gotten in the car. Mac drove recklessly, honking at the partiers to move while Heather worked the equipment.

"Got something," Heather said. "Getting better. Hey, pull over."

"Yeah just like that." He scanned the street, finally working the SUV next to a hydrant just off Duval Street. He moved his eyes to the screen. The camera was focused on a urinal. The audio was worthless once they'd entered the bar. Impossible to hear conversation, so Heather had turned it off. Mac thought for a second, trying to put himself into Trufante's twisted mind, then motioned toward Heather.

"Turn the audio back on."

Heather hit the button until they could hear. Trufante was humming. *Idiot*, Mac thought, until he realized what the song was. *Boom boom, Out Go the Lights.* Mac couldn't remember the name of the song, but the meaning was clear: they were going to the terrorists.

"Heather, call Jules, tell her to get out of there ahead of them. They're going to the terrorists."

She tried her own number from the burner phone. "I can't get her."

"Crap. Stay here. I'm going to see if I can find him." He was out of the car hobbling toward Duval Street. He spotted the bar he thought they were in and pushed through the line right past the bouncer. Two men from security followed. He quickly lost the men on the dance floor. Mac turned and spotted Mel on the bar, looking for a way down. He pushed toward her, playing the part of a jealous boyfriend as he moved people out of his way.

He yelled for her, trying to get her attention. She saw him and started strutting in his direction. He reached up to help her, but his leg couldn't take the weight. Fortunately, the crowd was thick enough to support them and hold them upright. They held each other for support as they moved toward the bathrooms. There was no way to cross the barrier of flesh when they saw Cesar frogmarch Trufante towards an emergency exit.

Mac caught Jules eye and signaled for her to follow. They pushed through the crowd heading to the exit.

Chapter 45

Outside the bar, Mac scanned the street, but there was no sign of them. "Call Heather. Maybe she has something," Jules said.

Mac handed her the phone, his face clouded with pain and two shades paler than usual.

Jules took the burner, flipped it open, and redialed the last number. "Hey, babe, you still got them?" The look on her face made it clear that the answer was negative. "What do we do now?"

"We'll never find them in this mess." He looked around at the crowds lining the sidewalks and spilling into the street. Cars were backed up as far as he could see. "Back to the car. We need to stay together and regroup. Heather picked them up once, she can do it again." Mac said as he moved forward, his limp worse.

Mac led the girls back to the SUV, wincing in pain every time his foot hit the ground. When they reached the car, Jules took the wheel and tried to pull out, honking at the couple making out in the driveway behind them. It was gridlock.

"We're two blocks from the end of the street. We should be able to set up a search grid — maybe four blocks each side of Duval," Heather said.

"That's really reaching. With this crowd it could take an hour to search four blocks," Jules said.

"Slow down," Mac said. We need a better plan than this."

"Let me have a look at that leg while we're waiting," Mel moved towards him.

Mac lifted his leg onto the seat. He flinched when she touched the T-shirt wrapped around the wound. "That bad?"

"It's already infected." She prodded the bright red areas,

"We need to get you to a hospital," Mel said.

"It can wait 'til this is over. We've got to get Trufante back and stop the terrorists. Heather, give her that stuff - it worked."

Heather handed the baggie to Mel. "Holy crap - is that what I think it is? Keep it down."

"The windows are tinted. Give me that," Mac said as he reached for the baggie. "Help me out here," he asked Mel.

"You can't put that back on there," Mel said as he went to rewrap the wound with the old bandage. "Here." She removed her T-shirt and tore a section of the fabric which she wound around the wound, securing it by pushing the end up and under the wrap.

They had only moved fifty feet when she finished. The pain gone now, Mac looked up and saw Heather texting. "Got something?"

"Garcia. He's staked out at the terrorist's house."

"Get the address, I bet that's where they're headed," Mac said.

"How are we going to get through this?" Mel asked.

"Drive," she told Heather. Jules stepped out of the car and Heather slid into the driver's seat. Jules was in front of the car, badge held high. They could hear her from inside the car - with the windows closed. She gestured at both vehicles and people, creating a space for the SUV.

* * *

They sat idling two blocks away from the address Garcia had given Heather. Mac and Mel got out and went towards the house. Heather pulled out, did a three-point U-turn and headed the other way. They held hands, trying to look like a couple out for a casual stroll as they cased the house. Mac wanted his own surveillance before meeting Garcia.

Lights were on in most rooms, but there was no sign of occupants as they walked past. They continued for another four houses, then crossed the street and came back on the other side.

Nothing had changed as they walked past again, then slid into the bougainvilleas bordering the neighbor's house.

Garcia was sitting in a squat, watching the house. He didn't turn as they pulled in next to him, but handed Mel his phone. "Send yourself a blank text. You'll have my number then. We can use that to communicate. No more voice after this. They have a 55-gallon drum in the garage they're making into a bomb. I believe the material is still in the house — they're in there now. Why don't you two go on the other side of the garage, see if you can see what they're up to. Remember, text only."

"Great, another cowboy. What is it with you guys not calling for help," she asked.

"I've seen the help around here, believe me when I tell you we are better off ourselves. On top of that it would take them hours to get it together. I think we only have minutes. I alerted Homeland Security to beef up security at the president's speech site."

"The president?" Mel gasped.

"Not now. Trust me ... just go."

Mac and Mel crept out of the bushes and walked down the street again, arm in arm this time. They passed the house and crept up to the garage. The position was more exposed than Mac would have liked, but he had no choice if they were to see inside the garage.

Mel texted Garcia: "Ready." She was facing the street, trying to shield the light from her phone from being visible when she saw two silhouettes approach. She knew it was Trufante from the man's size and gait. The smaller man was obviously Cesar. She pushed Mac to the side as they approached. He gave her a questioning look, then saw what she was pointing at, and they quickly retreated behind the garage. Mel texted Garcia about the men approaching and waited for his response. Once two men had passed by, Mac nudged her back to their original spot.

Garcia texted back that they were in the house now. That

made the odds steeper, with Cesar there. They knew he would be armed, and that he wasn't scared to shoot. "Sit and wait," Garcia texted Mel.

* * *

Ibrahim gave Cesar a questioning look. "The material is correct. What can I do for you?"

"Not so fast, *Abraham*. What's your timetable? I will not stop you if you tell me when and where. Let us get off the island, though, and you're free to pursue your twisted goals."

"I cannot tell you anything. Only Allah knows all."

Patel came down the stairs, dressed in the hazmat suit. "Who are these men? What are they doing here?"

"I am getting rid of them now."

"Wait. We need them to transport the barrel. It is more than we can do alone. I heard what he wants." He turned to Cesar. "You help us get everything in place and I will make sure you have ample time to leave."

Cesar nodded. "Deal, man. What's the plan?"

"You have a boat?" He watched as Cesar nodded. "I will tell you when we need your help. Until then," Patel motioned to the couch.

* * *

"What was that about the president?" Jules asked.

"He's here." Garcia glanced at his watch. "Giving a speech at the Truman White House in a couple of hours. I'm thinking that's where all this is going to end up."

"You don't need me here. Let Heather and I go to the site and check it out." This was too close to home for her to trust the bumbling Feds. She knew the area and the threat, giving her an advantage.

"Okay, stay in touch."

Chapter 46

A quick flash of her badge gave Jules access to the site. Even at five a.m. there was activity. Revelers were staggering by on their way home from the bars, watching as rental trucks lined up, quickly dumping their contents and leaving. The Truman White House was the perfect location for the speech. Located on Front Street, just blocks from Duval and many of the resorts, President Truman's retirement residence had been converted to a museum. The location allowed for most wanting to attend to get there on foot or via bicycle. Selected for it's size, the space would look like a large crowd, but in fact was small enough to easily control. The time was carefully picked. Friday morning at nine a.m. would eliminate most of the drunks, who would be sleeping off the night before. In Key West, you couldn't tell a Tuesday night from a Saturday night.

She texted Garcia that they were there. Heather used her phone to take pictures until they started getting suspicious glances from the Secret Service. They circled the house, and it quickly became apparent that the most likely place to launch an attack would be from the water. The boat basin's entry was unprotected, at least for now. Jules hoped that the Navy or Coast Guard would soon block the entrance to casual boaters.

* * *

Cesar watched with curiosity as the two men assembled the bomb. Although it insulted even his sadistic tendencies toward more personal torture, he was still interested. After all, you never knew when you might need to build a nuke. His violence was geared towards individuals who got in his way - not masses of innocents. They were in the garage, the interior warming quickly as the sun hit the metal roof. Patel dumped bags of ball bearings into the barrel with Ibrahim's help. He went back to the house and returned with a canister surrounded in bubble wrap. This was carefully placed in the center of the barrel and the remaining ball bearings were added around it.

"You think about who's going to lift that thing?" Cesar spurted.

Patel tried to tip the barrel, but it was too heavy. "You're right. We need to make it lighter."

"You got a freaking nuke sitting there! You don't need shrapnel. Put it on its side and dump it out. Leave some if you want, but that thing's got to be less than two hundred pounds or it'll capsize the boat. It'll be hard enough as it is to keep it balanced, and I ain't driving that mother fucker," Cesar said.

The four men carefully set the barrel on its side, sweeping the ball bearings out with their hands.

"Now, how are we gonna get this out of here?"

"I'll be back," Ibrahim said. "I have a truck rented. The rental place opens at seven." He glanced at his watch. "Almost time."

"Better if I go. You're too suspicious," Cesar said. "I know the dude at the rental place. Maybe I can get him there earlier. Watch him." He pointed to Trufante.

Ibrahim opened the garage door and pulled out his scooter. He looked toward Patel, who shook his head no. Ibrahim kicked the starter and pulled onto the street, heading back toward Duval. The streets were empty now, dawn on the horizon. He cruised back to Greene and turned left, heading toward the truck rental.

* * *

Mel sat on the ground. She leaned back and texted Garcia what was happening in the garage, as relayed by Mac, who was several feet off the ground in a tree, able to see through a window unobscured by the low bushes. It looked like they were finished with the assembly. Then the garage door opened suddenly, and Ibrahim left on the scooter. Mel sent an update to Garcia, who responded for them to stay with the bomb.

Mac crawled out of the tree and went to Mel. "Maybe we should try and get Trufante out of there now. They're just waiting."

"Let me see." Mel went to the window. She turned back to Mac in shock, "Oh my freakin' God - that's Patel. Crap, I knew that guy was bad."

Mac ignored her. He didn't care who was in there. His mind was focussed on two things: getting Trufante out and diffusing the bomb. "They've got to be paranoid and tired. They've been up all night. Maybe we could create a diversion and get him out of there. Stay here, let me see what I can come up with."

She moved to follow. "I'm going with you."

"Okay. Follow my lead."

* * *

"Tell Garcia we're coming over."

Mac peered around the side of the garage. Finding no one in sight, he stepped out quickly, heading away from the house. Mel followed, and they crossed the street together. The truck took them by surprise, barreling down the road way faster than the fifteen-mph speed limit. It hit a pothole and bounced, but the driver kept going. They stood on the sidewalk and stared, catching the eye of the driver before Mac realized what was happening and dove for cover.

He landed on his shoulder and screamed out in pain. A dog answered, barking as it ran toward them. The dog itself was not a problem, but the noise and activity would give away their location. The truck braked and stopped in front of the driveway. Cesar ran from the garage towards them. He drew his gun as he approached. The dog led him right to the couple.

"Out of there," he snapped.

Mac nodded at Mel, who went out first. He looked out of the corner of his eye and saw Garcia walk calmly up to Cesar, gun pointed at his head.

"Drop it, now. Set the gun down and kick it toward me."

Cesar complied, cursing under his breath.

"Now on your knees." Garcia was going for a zip tie to hand cuff Cesar when the first bullet struck him in the back. He went down on the asphalt, blood quickly formed a stream leading to the gutter.

Patel emerged from the garage, gun pointed at the group. "Amateurs. All of you inside."

They left Garcia in the street and walked single file to the garage. "Ibrahim, back the truck up. Cesar, tie them up. Then drag that body somewhere out of sight," Patel ordered.

The truck sounded an alarm as it backed into the driveway, and the dog continued to bark. The beeping stopped as Ibrahim set the parking brake and now it was just the dog barking.

Patel calmly crossed the street. One shot and the street was quiet again. "Filthy animals," he muttered to himself as he crossed back toward the house. He motioned them into the garage with the gun. Trufante was still there sitting in a corner, nursing his finger. "Phones, please. Cesar, get the FBI agent's when you move him." They tossed their phones on the floor. Patel removed the batteries, then smashed each with the butt of his gun. Cesar walked back with Garcia's phone and followed Patel's lead, his cowboy boot smashing the phone into pieces.

"Now, tie them up, all three of them," he said, pointing the gun at Mac, Mel and Trufante.

"We need the Cajun," Cesar said. It's going to take more than the three of us to move that thing.

Chapter 47

"Her phone's off. It's going straight to voicemail," Jules said. She set the phone down and started the engine. "We've got two hours before this shindig starts. Let's go get the boat. They're going to come in by water. I'm not sitting here and waiting for some alphabet agency guy to tell me what to do. This is our home."

"What about Mel and Mac?" Heather asked.

Jules thought for a minute, "If we don't stop the bomb, they're all dead anyway. We need to take care of the big picture. Mac is pretty creative, we've got to trust him."

The SUV pulled out from the curb, and she made the dock in minutes — a drive that would have taken half an hour during any time other than early morning. When they pulled up to the dock, Mac's boat was bobbing a quarter mile out, swinging on its anchor line, bow toward land with the outgoing tide.

"How are we going to get out there?"

"I have no idea how he got here." They looked around for transport, anything to get them out there. Heather went out to the dock and saw the paddleboard tied by a surf leash to a piling under the dock. "That's how." She pointed to the board.

"That's your deal, sister. I'm the golfer in the family."

Heather sat on the dock and used her feet to maneuver the board parallel to the structure. She'd been on a stand up board before, but the water had been calm. Once situated she sat on the dock and set one foot at a time on the board, got on her knees, and untied the velcro closure that held the leash to the piling. Paddle in hand, she stood and started pulling towards the boat. The water was choppy from the wind now, but the outgoing tide was in her favor, making each stroke count for two. She almost overran the boat, unable to steer in the chop. After a moment of panic a few hard strokes on the right turned the board towards Mac's boat. She got on the dive platform and dragged the board over the transom. The engines started, she raised the anchor, and idled toward the dock.

"Nice work," Jules said as she hopped over the transom. "You comfortable running this thing?"

"Yeah, if you can navigate."

Jules used her phone to pull up a Key West map and directed Heather out of the harbor and then west, following the coast until they went under the Fleming Key bridge and headed out to open water They went around a small island and slowed.

"Let's scout it out for a few and decide what to do here," Jules muttered. She dialed Mel's number again. The voicemail picked up before the phone could ring. "It's not even ringing. They're in trouble."

"We've got to prioritize. If this bomb goes off, there's no saving any of us."

* * *

Patel, Ibrahim, Cesar, and Trufante were squeezed into the front of the truck. No one spoke as Ibrahim shifted into reverse and pulled out of the driveway, looking at the house for the last time. He'd lingered in the garage taking the diluted radioactive mixture Mac had made and added the shrapnel scattered on the garage floor to an old steel gas can with about a gallon left. He placed the can in a pan, which he had filled with muriatic acid. This second bomb would easily blow the entire block. It would take an hour for the acid to eat through the rusted can, allowing the chemicals to mix, but the beauty of the smaller bomb was that no one would know if there were more or not. Terrorism was at its most effective when people were scared into altering their behavior.

The truck moved slowly down the street, this time obeying the speed limit, Ibrahim swerving to avoid potholes. Even with the drum secured to the side of the truck, if it spilled and dumped its contents, the plan was ruined. Cesar directed them to the marina, where his boat was dry docked. Ten minutes later they pulled into the parking area. There was activity even at this early hour as a steady stream of fishermen prepared their boats and left the basin. Cesar directed the attendant to retrieve his boat. Minutes later, the forklift slid underneath the yellow and red hull of the cigarette boat and lifted it out of the rack. The lift rolled to the dock and set the boat in the water.

"Hurry! Ibrahim, back up the truck. The fewer people who see us load this, the better," Patel snapped.

"Not a big deal," Cesar said. "It's pretty common around here to see folks going out with drums. They don't know it's full, or what's in it. These yahoos will think we're taking it out empty to make a lobster haven. They dump crap out there all the time." He looked at the two terrorists, "Can you two not look so freakin' guilty?"

The truck backed up and the four men wrestled the drum off the tailgate. Cesar and Trufante rolled it on its edge down the dock, and waited for Ibrahim and Patel to help lift it onto the boat.

The combined weight of the drum and the four men all in one corner almost swamped the boat and Cesar cringed when the hull scraped against a piling, leaving a yellow streak on the old wood. Once the barrel was loaded, they separated, allowing the boat to regain its equilibrium.

"Start it up. Let's get out of here," Patel said.

"This is as far as we go. You said load it, that's it."

"Not so fast. We have one more stop to make. You think I am on a suicide mission here? We will be well away when the explosion occurs." Patel drew his gun and placed it by his leg — out of sight to any onlookers, but visible to Cesar.

They idled out of the marina, then, impatient but careful to stay at idle speed. The last thing they wanted was to attract the attention of nearby boats by creating a wake. The engines were loud, even at an idle, as they wove through the boats and into the channel. Once clear of the last buoy, Cesar pushed the throttle down and the boat lurched forward.

"What are you doing?" Patel yelled over the engines. "Slow down. We hit one wave the wrong way and this will be a suicide mission!"

Cesar slowed to fifteen knots. Too slow to get the boat up on plane, it churned through the water.

"You don't want to arouse suspicion. Any one looking at this boat going so slow will think either something's wrong, or an idiot is driving it. We're sure to attract attention."

"That gives me an idea," Ibrahim said. "Here, take the wheel." Trufante took over the helm as he went back to the engine compartment, lifted the hatch, and started reaching around in the dark hole to find the oil fill plug. Once removed, the vibration of the engine and action of the waves caused oil to splatter out of the hole and hit the engine block. The hot engine immediately started to smoke. Satisfied, he came back up to eye level and admired the stream of smoke trailing the boat.

They continued their slow pace towards the target, the smoke and speed making them look like they'd blown an engine. Ibrahim watched the other boats, most obscured by the smoke screen.

Chapter 48

Mac and Mel were prone on the floor, hands and feet tied behind their backs, duct tape covering their mouths. The metal roof on the garage absorbed the heat and the garage was starting to heat up as the sun climbed the sky. They watched through watering eyes as the muriatic acid smoked, slowly eating away at the gas can. When the acid ate through the rusty metal, they both knew what would happen. Ibrahim had set the pan at eye level to insure they could watch the tool of their demise.

Their only means of communication was their eyes. Mac looked toward the workbench, unable to see the top of it from the floor, and started to fidget. After a moment, he found that he could move like an inchworm. He motioned his head at Mel, signaling that he was going to work his way there and that she should follow. They both inched toward the bench, hoping there was something they could use to cut the duct tape binding them. Mac reached the bench first and tried to rise. The pain from his leg was unbearable. He made it to his knees, then fell, unable to balance enough to gain his feet. His leg was throbbing as the anesthetic effect of the coke had worn off hours ago.

As if the pain was not enough, the duct tape made it difficult to breathe. Hyperventilating from exertion and the accumulating smoke was letting his mind go where it shouldn't. No time to panic, he tried to steady his breath, his dive training automatically taking over. As he calmed, he noticed glue from the tape rubbing against the five-day growth of beard. It was making his mouth itch, but it gave him an idea. He rubbed the tape against his shoulder and noticed a slight pull. Repeating the movement several more times pulled a corner of the tape from his face, and then slid against the leg of the workbench, pushing his face against the leg. It took several tries before the tape grabbed. He turned his head slowly, the tape partially tearing from his mouth. It worked until his neck's range of motion gave out. He would need to spin his body around to get the remainder of the tape off, but it was a start.

He glanced over at Mel, who was trying the same thing. The tape adhered to her smooth skin better than Mac's rough face, and he tried to reassure her with his eyes as he readied himself. He figured he'd only have one shot at this. If the tape came off the table leg, there wouldn't be enough adhesive left to stick it back. He breathed in and released all the air from his lungs. Every joint ached in protest as they were strained past their norm, but he was able to balance enough with his feet together in a squat position to spin in place. The last of the tape came off and he collapsed on the floor, screaming in pain as he hit the concrete.

He regained his breath and moved toward Mel. Their heads came together, and his teeth tore at the tape. Then they both sat back and took a deep breath. After a moment, the urgency of their situation took hold, as the acid etched into the rusty metal of the gas can. They had no idea how much time they had before it gave way; the smallest pinhole would accelerate the process as gasoline met acid.

"We've got to get out of here," Mel said.

"You got that right. One of us needs to get our hands free to open the door, though." He looked at the bench. "If I can get up to the bench, there's bound to be something there we can use." He tried to stand again, but his restraints made balance impossible. "Can you slide under me and prop me up?"

She inched towards him and tried to kneel as he stood. Just as his eyes reached the bench and saw the blade of a drywall knife, he toppled over backwards and smacked his head against the floor.

"That hurt. Crap. But there's a small saw on the table. If we get that, I can hold it with my teeth and cut you free."

Suddenly the pan hissed. They both turned and watched the

smoke increase.

"We've got to try again. Now," Mel snapped.

They set themselves up as before and he tried to rise again. As he reached the crux, he felt his balance start to go. He did the only thing he could and grabbed for the table edge with his mouth, his teeth digging into the old wood top. It gave him enough leverage to stand. He spat out the wood and moved for the saw. It was about eight inches long, a keyhole saw, with a rough, serrated blade and a wood handle. He got the handle situated in his mouth and went to his knees.

Gas was clearly starting to mix with the acid now, and the fumes caused them both to cough. Their vision became obscured as well, eyes watering from the smoke. Mac tried to keep his cool as he got in position behind Mel and started to saw the duct tape. She screamed in pain with every stroke as he was unable to control the end of the blade. Small rivulets of blood started streaming down her arms, but she didn't complain and he didn't apologize. He finally figured out that the saw cut better moving backwards rather than forward, and the tape began to fall away. Two more pulls and she was free.

"Give it to me."

Mel retrieved the saw where if fell and quickly cut her feet. Then she turned to Mac and cut his hands. He shook them to get the circulation back and took the saw from her. It quickly tore through the tape at his ankles. His feet freed, they both ran for the door and pulled it open together. It lifted a few inches and stopped.

"He must have jammed it from the outside. Go for the window."

They dove through the window and rolled, landing awkwardly, but outside. "We've got to put it out. I'll open the door. Did you see a fire extinguisher in there?" Mac yelled.

"No, want me to check the house?" Mel asked.

"It's probably locked. Break a window if you have to," he responded.

Chapter 49

At the wheel of the drifting boat, Trufante was staring at his finger, when the wake came from nowhere and hit the side of the cigarette boat. Built for speed, the boat had a narrow beam. Built longer and narrower than most boats, it was great for racing, but the tradeoff was stability. The barrel tipped in its restraint as the boat turned nearly on its side, as Patel and Ibrahim ran over to support it. The added weight from the men in the corner of the boat caused it to tip even more.

Trufante was paying attention now, looking for the source of the wake, "A cruise ship. She's coming into the pier."

"Allah has blessed us further," Patel said. "There must be several thousand infidels aboard."

"Son of a bitch." Trufante stared at the boat.

Their boat was adrift behind Sunset Key. Trufante looked at the resort, guest houses dotting the white sand beach. They were sitting idle apparently killing time, although he didn't know how long they had. He eyed the small island again trying to determine if the distance was swimmable.

"We need to get this thing off here before something else goes wrong. You guys got a plan, or are we going to just drive the boat into the dock?" Cesar asked as he glanced over at the two terrorists, both praying. Neither answered. Trufante caught his eye. "Hey, Cajun. Help me tie the barrel down better. I wouldn't want anything to go wrong now. Can one of you take the wheel?"

Patel moved toward the helm as Cesar slid behind him. Ibrahim moved forward as well, allowing Trufante access to the rear of the boat. The two men huddled around the barrel, checking the tie-downs. Trufante leaned over to Cesar and whispered, "We gotta go. Jump and swim for the island."

He nodded. They continued to fuss with the straps as Cesar glanced forward. Both men were entranced by the cruise ship sent by Allah, and Cesar nudged Trufante and dove off the transom. Trufante took off after him.

"Follow me," Trufante said. His experience in the water was vastly better than Cesar's, and he instantly judged the current and swam with it. The outgoing tide worked in their favor, bringing them closer to the island, but Cesar was in trouble. He struggled as the waves crashed over his head, taking in water with each breath. "Coast with the waves. On your side. Breathe at the top and stop looking back."

Trufante treaded water and watched him. "You got to lose the boots dude. They're drowning you."

"No way, Cajun," He spat water.

* * *

"It's all I could find." She handed the bag of kitty litter to him.

"Good thinking. It should work." Mac set the gas can on the bench and opened the cap to pour the granules in. He kept pouring until the hole was full, praying that it would be enough. With luck, the sand would absorb the gas and keep it inside the can. Removed from the acid, the can seemed intact, and he didn't see any evidence of the gas having run into the acid itself.

He looked up at Mel, relieved. "Think that's it. The bomb squad can take it from here. Did you notice a land line in the house?"

Mel shook her head. "I'll check again."

"Don't bother, we know where they're going."

He looked around the garage, focusing on an old tandem bicycle hanging upside down from its wheels. "Hey, help me get this down."

They went to the old bike and lifted it off the hooks. It had been sitting so long that the rims touched the ground through the the flat tires. Mel dug through the shelves and came back with a foot pump. The tires eagerly accepted the air, and the bike rose off the ground.

"Don't know if they'll hold, but it's better than walking," Mac said.

They pulled the bike into the driveway and exchanged a look about who should steer. "You know the island better," Mel conceded.

It was sketchy for a minute until they found their rhythm, but once they did, the bike was fast. They went out to North Roosevelt and turned left. The boat harbor came quickly into view on the left, and Mac stopped short of the entrance, almost throwing Mel from the bike.

Mac navigated the parking lot, coming to a stop at the dock where he had left his board. They both dismounted at the seawall and Mac stared out to where his boat had been anchored, seeing nothing but water. He went down the pier and looked underneath for the paddleboard.

"Heather and Jules have the boat." He saw the black SUV parked. "The paddleboard's gone too. Should we just ride to Front Street and see what we can do from the land side?"

"If they've got the boat they know something we don't. It's going to happen from the water. We won't do any good on land." She looked around the parking lot. "Look, there's a two-seat outrigger canoe. We can get there in that, hopefully spot your boat."

"Never been in one."

"That's my gig, and I'm driving this time." They abandoned the bike and went for the canoe. Mel grabbed the cross-braces holding the float to the hull. "Grab the bow. We'll put in at the boat ramp." They carried the canoe and the outrigger to the edge of the water. "I got this. Find some paddles."

Mac went toward the boathouse where the canoes were stored, and dug around for two old wooden paddles. When he returned, Mel had attached the ama to the boat and slid it into the water. "Same stroke as your board. Get in front. I'll steer."

She pushed the bow toward open water and waited for him to get in. Once he had found his spot, she pushed off and hopped in the stern like the last guy in a bobsled. The canoe settled with their weight, and promptly died in the water.

Mac shook his head. "We gotta switch. We'll swamp with my weight in the front."

Mel reluctantly realized he was right. "Always have to be in charge." They switched positions, and Mel set her paddle and pulled. Mac, out of sync, set his, and the boat spun.

Mel turned around and glared at him. "Got to do this together. I'll stay on the right side, you on the left. On my call, now. And pull." She paused while they stroked, then called it again. They started to get into a rhythm, and the boat glided forward.

"Sucker's fast," Mac muttered, watching the land slide by.

"Shut up and paddle."

* * *

Trufante reached the beach first. He lay on the sand, catching his breath, his finger stinging from the salt water. Cesar was still fifty yards off shore, struggling to reach the beach. By the time his feet touched ground, Trufante was standing and ready to go.

Cesar crawled onto shore and crossed himself. "Goddamn, Cajun, that was hard." Water dripped from his boots.

"We need a boat. You coming?"

"Yeah, give me a minute."

Trufante didn't wait. He started walking toward the street and turned left. "There's a marina around the corner here. We need to get there."

He had to turn around and check on Cesar several times as they walked. The Mexican was struggling, bent over, gasping for air. He waited patiently, stopping several times until a small pier came into view. Two security guards stood outside a shack.

"What about them? This is some fancy resort. They're going to look at us and put the cuffs on before they ask for a room key," Cesar snorted.

"Leave the talking to me."

They walked toward the marina, leaving a trail of water from their drenched clothes. As they approached, Trufante took the lead. A dive boat sat at the pier, tanks strapped to each side. It was idling, but no crew was in sight. *Probably organizing the divers,* thought Trufante. That was the boat he wanted. He went to the dock and met the look of the first guard.

"Hey, man, the boat ready?"

"Excuse me? Are you a guest?" The guard eyed him carefully.

"No, man. Name's Alan Trufante, but you can call me Tru," he grinned. "They hired me and my boy here." He pointed to Cesar. "Got a wreck they want to dive on. Asked us to take them out to it. Kind of a special deal, you know, not on the charts, and I ain't giving up the GPS numbers to nobody. In fact, I'd appreciate if you checked the crew and guests for handheld devices and confiscate their cell phones. They'll dig it, man. Make it seem top secret." Trufante winked at him.

The guard, still suspicious, went to his partner and spoke in hushed tones. He came back. "No one told us about you."

"Top secret, like I said. These cats are paying big bucks for this. Word gets out that old Tru is showing off his honey hole, there'd be spies everywhere." He shaded his brow and looked around. "You boys seen any suspicious activity?"

They both shook their heads, and Trufante walked right by

them to the boat. "Remember to collect their phones," he yelled over his shoulder as he headed to the boat.

Cesar was ten yards behind him grinning. "Damn, Cajun, That was a line of shit. Serious, *hombre*."

They both hopped onboard. "Look busy. Like you're checking tanks and stuff. Toss the lines while you're at it." Trufante went to the helm and revved the engine while Cesar untied the bow line and moved towards the stern. Trufante looked toward the guards and saw them confiscating the phones from a couple of passengers. Then two men in matching uniforms approached the guards. They talked briefly, and the four men quickly headed toward the boat. The guards drew their guns as Trufante reversed to the edge of the dock, but it was too late. Trufante had seen them and realized it was time to go. He pushed the throttle forward and shot away from the dock. Bullets hit the water, and Trufante and Cesar looked at each other and started laughing.

"How far can this thing take us?"

"Probably get up to Key Largo, but it'll be a slow ride. This thing ain't built for speed. Or bumps."

"*Amigo*, let's get the hell out of here."

Chapter 50

Mac and Mel had a good rhythm going as they rounded the breakwater and passed the ferry pier. The canoe was cruising through the light chop, spray flying into their faces. He was initially frustrated as she tried to teach him how to switch sides on her call every fifteen strokes or so. Mac was used to paddling his stand up boards and not used to taking direction. He eventually came around to her call after seeing how much faster the boat moved when they were in rhythm. His leg ached as he tried to find a comfortable position. The cruise ship dock appeared in the distance and Mac slowed his stroke and steered them into the basin of the Pier House Resort.

"We gotta regroup and make some kind of a plan. It's just past that cruise ship. We can't just paddle in there, unarmed, and think we're going to save the day," Mac said

"You're right. Got any ideas?" she answered.

"I don't even know what boat they're using. All we can do is keep going. Sitting here is not getting us anywhere."

"Agreed."

They started paddling, the bow pointed toward Sunset Key. Suddenly they saw a dive boat moving toward them. Mac stopped again. Trufante stood out even at this distance.

"That's Trufante and that drug dealer. I'm sure of it." He waved his paddle in the air.

* * *

Trufante squinted into the sun. The paddle waving in the air caught his attention — an almost sure sign of distress. Surprised to see Mac in the back of the canoe, he changed course slightly so as not to alert Cesar, knowing he only had seconds to figure out a plan before he overtook his friends. He glanced around the deck of the boat. The pontoon boat was about forty-feet long and almost fifteen-feet wide, built for the easy five-mile run to the reef in light seas. Each pontoon had an outboard at its end. The Yamaha 115-HP motors were enough to bring the boat onto plane in calm seas and churn through the chop. The deck had benches down each side with scuba tanks strapped behind them.

Without another option, Trufante slid his hand below the wheel and turned the key to the port engine off. The boat immediately started to swing into a left turn.

"Crap, we lost an engine. Take the wheel and I'll have a look." He slowed the starboard engine to an idle and stepped away from the controls. Cesar took over and Trufante walked toward the stern. He'd bought a little time, but still had no plan. He went to the port side and fumbled with the engine, taking the cowling off, and exposing the guts. The canoe was moving closer. He was running out of time.

"Hurry up!" Cesar yelled. "That freaking bomb could blow us clear of here any time now!"

"Working on it." Trufante stood and looked around. A tank was all he had, so he grabbed one from the rack. "Gotta blow some crap out of the line."

"Just hurry up."

He took the tank to the engine and opened the valve. Cesar was preoccupied with trying to keep the boat running straight on one engine, giving Trufante the time he needed. He stood and went toward the helm, the force of the compressed air reaching Cesar well before Trufante did. He struggled against it, his eyes closed against the rush of air. Trufante saw his moment and swung the tank into Cesar's head.

He watched him fall to the deck and said goodbye to his

fortune smuggling drugs through the bayou. A pool of blood was already starting to form as he shut off the tank and replaced the cowling on the engine.

The canoe pulled up alongside him as he wiped the sweat from his brow. Mel was first to hop onto the boat. Mac followed behind her, and pushed the canoe into the current.

"He deserved that," Mel said looking at the body as she took the wheel.

"Nice work." Mac pounded him on the back. "Where's the bomb? We can catch up on the story later."

"Cigarette boat. Those two terrorists are waiting out there." He pointed. "They're drifting off the back of the island."

"Let's go," Mac said motioning to Cesar's body. "Help me with him." They both fought to keep their footing in the blood pooled on the deck as they dragged the body to the side. Mac slipped and smashed his injured calf into the gunwale.

"I got it." Trufante went to the transom and turned on the freshwater wash-down used by the divers to rinse off after a dive. As he sprayed the deck, the blood formed into rivulets before forming a creek, and then a stream. He started to hose the body down.

"Whoa, hold up." Mac looked at the tattoo covering Cesar's arms. He crawled over and shook his head, pursing his lips as if he had found something of value.

"Head us over there," He yelled to Mel. "Do they know what kind of boat you're in?" He asked Trufante.

"Don't think so. We jumped off theirs, made it to the island there, and stole this."

He looked around at the other boats all heading to sea. "Well, let's look like we're just heading toward the reef like everyone else and see what they're up to."

The dive boat rounded the island, and Trufante pointed toward the cigarette boat. "That's them."

Mac looked at his watch. "The speech starts in ten minutes. They're going to start moving any second. The only thing we can do is sink it."

"How?"

"Cesar got a gun?" Mac asked. Trufante shook his head, but Mac went to the body anyway, again glancing at the ink. He rolled the drug runner over and checked, but found no gun.

"Slow down," he called to Trufante. He pointed toward the shore. "There. That's where we'll make our move."

Trufante swung the boat and headed for the stern of the cruise boat. There was a narrow opening there, where the cigarette boat would be forced to travel close to the ship on its way in.

"We're going to stay a hundred yards off the cruise ship and wait. I don't think either of those guys have the balls to drive that thing full throttle through the cut. We try and run up alongside them and toss a couple of tanks into their boat. I'm counting on them being slow to react."

"What's that going to do?" Mel asked.

"Just watch. Can you drive? I need Tru."

Mac was on his knees, unlatching the clips that held the bench in place. "Tru, help me here." Each bench was eight feet long, with metal legs attached to the deck. Behind each bench were sections of plastic pipe for the dive tanks to sit in.

"Pull the tanks out," Mac muttered. Trufante removed the six tanks from behind the bench, and laid them down on the deck. Then they pulled the first bench away from the gunwale, setting it to the side and going to work on the plastic pipes behind. The six pieces were secured to a piece of plywood that was screwed to the boat.

Mac looked up at Mel. "Babe, are there any tools in that compartment below?" She bent over to search, and Mac looked out at the other boat moving closer. They would have to hurry.

"Just a few screwdrivers."

"Toss 'em over."

Mac and Tru each grabbed a screwdriver and went to work on the screws. Once those were out, they pulled the plywood free and set it on the gunwale. The tank holders were on their side now, looking like portholes. Mac and Trufante smiled at each other.

Chapter 51

"Time to go, my friend. Have you made your peace with Allah?" Patel asked.

"Yes, my brother. And you?"

"Paradise will be bountiful for the soldiers of Allah."

Ibrahim pushed the throttle down half way and headed toward the cut.

* * *

Mac grinned when he saw the boat start to move. Not only were they going to slow down through the cut, they were going to idle the entire way in. He had guessed correctly that they would not try it at full speed. "Ready?"

"Yeah." She applied downward pressure to the two throttles, and the boat slowly picked up speed. In a minute they would be even with the other boat.

* * *

The two boats were closing fast. Mac was ready, a tank at his feet. Trufante moved next to Mac, another tank ready at his side.

The boat was fifty feet away when Mel turned the wheel slightly to the left, allowing them to draw parallel. Carefully she matched the boat's speed as they inched closer.

"Now!" Mac yelled. Both men simultaneously lifted the tanks and inserted them in a tank holder. They were facing the cigarette boat, valves facing toward the boat. Ibrahim and Patel glanced over, fear in their eyes.

Mac picked up a weight belt, wound up, and smashed it into the valve. It shot backwards, almost taking him out.

"Crap. Set 'em the other way!" he shouted.

Trufante loaded the rack with five more tanks, valves facing out now, and Mac swung again. The valves released, hitting the other boat in the side. One penetrated the fiberglass and the other took Ibrahim in the stomach. The terrorist was thrown overboard, the velocity sinking him.

The cigarette boat was listing toward them now, the deck leaning up to the sky. Mac went back to the tanks and raised the weight belts again. Two more valves flew toward the boat. Both holed the hull. The boat was taking on water now, and Patel fell backwards landing against the barrel, still strapped to the boat.

Mac, Mel, and Trufante stood together on the dive boat and watched as water poured onto the deck, finally capsizing the cigarette boat.

The three exchanged glances, but there was no celebration.

"Full throttle!" Mac yelled.

Mel gave him a questioning look.

"Now!" He glanced over at the sinking boat. "The vortex from the boat going down will suck us in. We've got to get clear."

She pressed down on the controls, and the boat slowly moved forward, the outboards struggling against the pull of the water as the cigarette boat sank, along with its dangerous cargo. They could feel the suction break as the boat picked up speed. The vessel started to disappear beneath the water. The barrel remained buoyant, the last thing to sink, but finally the weight of the boat dragged it under. and the boat vanished.

Mel slowed as the water settled. Mac looked around to confirm they were clear. He went to Cesar's body, pulled him from beneath the bench and laid his arms out. "Toss me that camera." He pointed to a dive camera hanging from the console

Mel gave him a questioning look, but tossed it to him. Mac caught it and flipped it open. He hit the camera icon and started taking pictures of Cesar's arms. Once he'd gotten every angle, he examined the rest of his body. He checked the dead man's pockets and pulled out the cloth bag that Cesar had taken from his safe, felt the contents through the fabric, and stuffed it in his pants.

"What are you doing?" Mel asked.

"I'll explain later. We gotta get him over before anyone gets out here."

He took the weight belt and wrapped it around Cesar's waist. Trufante came over, and they dumped the body over the side. They were a quarter mile away from the spot the cigarette boat had gone down, and Mac was confident that no one would search here.

"Head out at a hundred and eighty degrees. Hopefully we can get caught up in the traffic heading to the reef and disappear." The boat swung toward the heading.

Suddenly Mel pointed over the windshield to the outline of a boat. "Mac, look, it's your boat. It must be Jules and Heather."

"You're right. Better be careful, though. We don't know it's them for sure." Two Coast Guard helicopters passed overhead in the direction of the wreck. Mac picked up the radio and dialed it to channel sixteen. The radio chatter was mostly law enforcement coordinating the cleanup. Even if Jules had the radio on, it was a bad idea to call on sixteen. He had an idea and went to channel seventy two. Jules answered on the private channel. Mac was sure their quick conversation on a side channel mostly used by fishermen would go unnoticed. A smile crossed his face. He went to Mel and hugged her. She leaned into him as she steered toward his boat, and he keyed the mic again. "Follow us out. We'll meet up in a mile or two." He shut the radio off.

They were three miles out, patch reefs visible below the boat, when they met. It took the extra mile to satisfy Mac that they wouldn't be observed. Jules slowed and tossed a line. Once aboard Mac's boat, they stared at each other, no one knowing how to break the silence.

"Come on, y'all, we saved the planet," Trufante said.

A quiet snicker turned into full belly laughs all around as the stress fell from their faces.

Mac broke the moment. "We gotta sink the dive boat. Leave no trace, as they say. Then we can head home." He pulled the line, bringing the boat closer. The gas and dive tanks still onboard were handed over the transom and stored. One last look around, and Mac came back aboard. He went down to the cabin and came back with a waterproof dry bag.

"Let me have the camera." Mel handed it over, and he placed it in the pouch and pressed the air out as he rolled the top back on itself, closing the seal. He hopped back on the dive boat, reached up under the console, and came out with a handful of wires. The dry bag tied securely, he called for a hammer. Trufante passed one to him. He went to work on the pontoons, walking down the length of the boat and puncturing them with the hammer as he went. The boat settled lower in the water, the holes starting to take on water. Finished, he jumped back over the transom and untied the line.

They watched as the boat disappeared from sight. Then Mac went to the helm and saved the GPS number before putting the boat in gear and heading east toward Marathon.

STEVEN BECKER

Epilogue

Sportsman's lobster season — first chance at the spiny lobster before the commercial fisherman set their traps, was the busiest weekend of the year. It was rare to find a vacant hotel, the restaurants were jammed, and the traffic on US 1 was suicidal. Mac picked this weekend on purpose. Only six weeks after sinking the dive boat, he was motoring back to the same site. He'd chosen this day for exactly what he loathed — people. Not sure if he was under surveillance, the only way to watch what he was going to do today was from a helicopter. And he'd be able to see one if it came after him.

They left shortly after sunrise, the time also picked to blend in. Mel and Trufante were aboard, sipping coffee as his boat cut through the flat, calm waters. Even the weather was in his favor this morning. Every conceivable vessel that could float would be able to get out today, making it a nightmare for the Coast Guard. Cruising at twenty knots the three-hour trip brought them in sight of Key West at nine a.m. — prime time for the lobster divers. The GPS directed him to the site, which was fortunately vacant.

"You can see the damned thing from here," Trufante said as he set the anchor on the thirty-foot-deep patch of reef.

"I don't want anyone close to us. The flag should give us some space." Mac ran the red-and-white striped dive flag up one of the outriggers, and started setting up equipment. "You and Mel do your best to keep everyone away. Whatever it takes." He set the first stage of the regulator on the tank, tightened the knob, and turned on the air. Minutes later, he was ready to go in the water. Then Trufante came out of the cabin with a bag.

"What's that for? I'm just getting the burner phone."

"There's critters down there. You want to blend in. Lemme

see you bring back a limit."

Mac took the bag, set the regulator in his mouth, and checked for air flow. He gathered the gauges into his body with one arm and put the other hand over the mask and regulator. Then he rolled in, the water splashing around him. Mel and Trufante watched him descend to the wreck from the boat above.

The wreck had a layer of barnacles already — the first of the many it would receive as it became a reef. Small fish darted out of his path as he clipped the dive bag to a section of rail and went toward the helm. He was about to flip on his back when he saw the antennae poking from the cavity. He laughed as he went for the bag and plucked four lobsters from the compartment under the wheel. With them safely in the bag, he secured it and went back to the hole. On his back, he removed a small dive light from a clip on his BC and shined it into the space. He slid his head in, scaring a school of bait-sized fish.

The light illuminated the cavity. The colors of the wires, covered with sea slime, were now barely distinguishable, but the dry bag dangled where he had tied it off six weeks ago. He breathed a sigh of relief as he went to work on the wires. Once loose, he pulled his body out of the hole and clipped the bag and his light to the BC.

He broke the surface of the water, "Here you go. Only four." He threw the bag to Trufante. "Hand me the blasting caps."

Trufante went below and handed Mac the four sticks of dynamite stuffed into two liter soda bottles. Mac had bought the explosives in Miami using his commercial salvage license, and it was cheaper to use standard explosives with a waterproof fuse and rig them through a bottle than use the more expensive underwater brand. There were also fewer questions asked.

Back in the water, he set a charge in each pontoon and another in the compartment under the helm. He was looking around for a place to set the last charge when the six-foot black fin shark cruised by him. He quickly lit the three fuses, set to detonate in ten minutes. He wanted enough time to get away, but not enough for someone else to anchor on the site. The shark cruised back again, nudging him as it got more aggressive. It circled again, this time with a tighter radius. Mac looked it in the eyes and knew it was keyed in on him. Swimming for the surface would only make him an easier target. He stood his ground.

The shark came back around, this time mouth open, heading straight for him. Mac pinched the fuse to an inch of the bottle cap, lit it, and pushed toward the surface. He looked back as the shark swung towards him, then flipped to face the open mouth and jammed the bottle in. Distracted and angry, the shark swam off and circled. At the apex of the circle, just as Mac broke the surface, the charge went off, causing the water to erupt. Blood and flesh were scattered along the surface as he climbed out.

"Get the anchor. Let's get out of here." He took the helm as the anchor chain locked into the bow pulpit. The boat shot forward as he pushed the throttles down. Seconds later, the water burst once, and twice more. He looked around to see if anyone was watching, but there was nothing to indicate anyone had the least interest in anything besides drinking beer and getting their limit of lobster.

* * *

Mac walked down the stairs from Heather's apartment, the flash drive in his pocket, and went to the dumpster to toss the camera in. Heather had removed the SIM card and transferred the pictures to the flash drive. She insisted on keeping a copy to update the gang tattoo database, but that was a small cost for something he wasn't equipped to do himself. He'd seen enough on her computer screen to get excited. The ancestral tattoos that covered the guy's arm were high quality, the pictures good enough to show the intricacies in the patterns that he was looking for.

Mel was working at her laptop when he entered the house. She'd carved out a permanent space in his kitchen for her work station.

"Got what you need?" she asked.

"Yeah. Can't wait to see if I can piece this thing together," he said.

"You going to tell me what all this is about?" Mel was getting frustrated by his elusiveness.

"I just want to add the next piece of the puzzle and it'll make more sense. Something your dad and I were working on."

She went back to the computer. "Hey, look at this." She angled the screen so they could both see the article, and he went to her side, draping an arm around her shoulder as they both read. The blog showed a picture of Davies leaving the federal courthouse in Washington in handcuffs, his lawyer holding a sheaf of papers in front of his face. They both read:

"Indicted on counts of obstructing justice, reckless endangerment, and fraud, attorney Bradley Davies was sentenced to five years at a minimum-security prison today."

"That's not nearly enough for what he almost cost this country, and I still feel bad about Garcia. For a Fed, he was alright," Mac said.

"I know, but from what I heard they didn't have enough evidence to go for treason. They went for the sure thing."

He shook his head. "At least he's ruined. The power meant more to him than the money, anyway."

"Amen." She leaned her head up to him and they kissed. "Well, it's over."

He looked over toward the bedroom, hoping that was where this was leading, but turned as the door opened.

"Y'all sitting here playing on the computer? We ought to be out grabbing some bugs or something. At least having a beer."

Mac nodded toward the refrigerator, not that Trufante needed an invitation.

"Tomorrow."

Get the real story of the square grouper in the author's note here: http://wp.me/p47V3Q-22

Thanks for Reading

For more information please check out my web page:
https://stevenbeckerauthor.com/

Or follow me on Facebook:
https://www.facebook.com/stevenbecker.books/

Made in the USA
Middletown, DE
10 October 2022

12473563R00142